ASHEN RIDER

A DUSK AND DAWN NOVEL

JAMES D. MILLS

THE ARCANIST: FANTASY PUBLISHING

The Arcanist: Fantasy Publishing, LLC

Bloomington, Indiana, United States.

Websites: thearcanist.net | magazine.thearcanist.net

Contact: business@thearcanist.net

Support: support@thearcanist.net

First serialized online: July 2025

First paperback and hardcover editions: December 2025

First ebook edition: December 2025

Paperback ISBN: 979-8-9923135-8-1
Hardcover ISBN: 979-8-9923135-9-8

DUSK AND DAWN

Standalone novels

Ashen Rider

Soil*

Phrygian Nights**

The Heretic's Reflection

What Lies Below*

Those Left Behind**

Anthologies

Threshold: Tales of Fantasy and Reality*

* (Forthcoming, 2026)

** (Forthcoming, 2027)

For Eden...

    Who ceaselessly challenges me to be the best man I can be.

Acknowledgement

Thank you, Lee Patton, for believing in this story and for the countless hours you spent with it.

Eternal Gratitude

A special thank you to my good friends Dane Bankston, Courtney Jensen, and Will Hager for supporting this book and its follow-ups on Kickstarter.

It means the world to me.

It matters not how strait the gate,

  How charged with punishments the scroll,
I am the master of my fate,

  I am the captain of my soul.

"Invicutus" by William Earnest Henley (1920).

THE OLD EMPIRE OF KALDEA

AS SHE STANDS IN THE ONE-HUNDRED AND THIRTY YEARS
AFTER ARRIVAL.

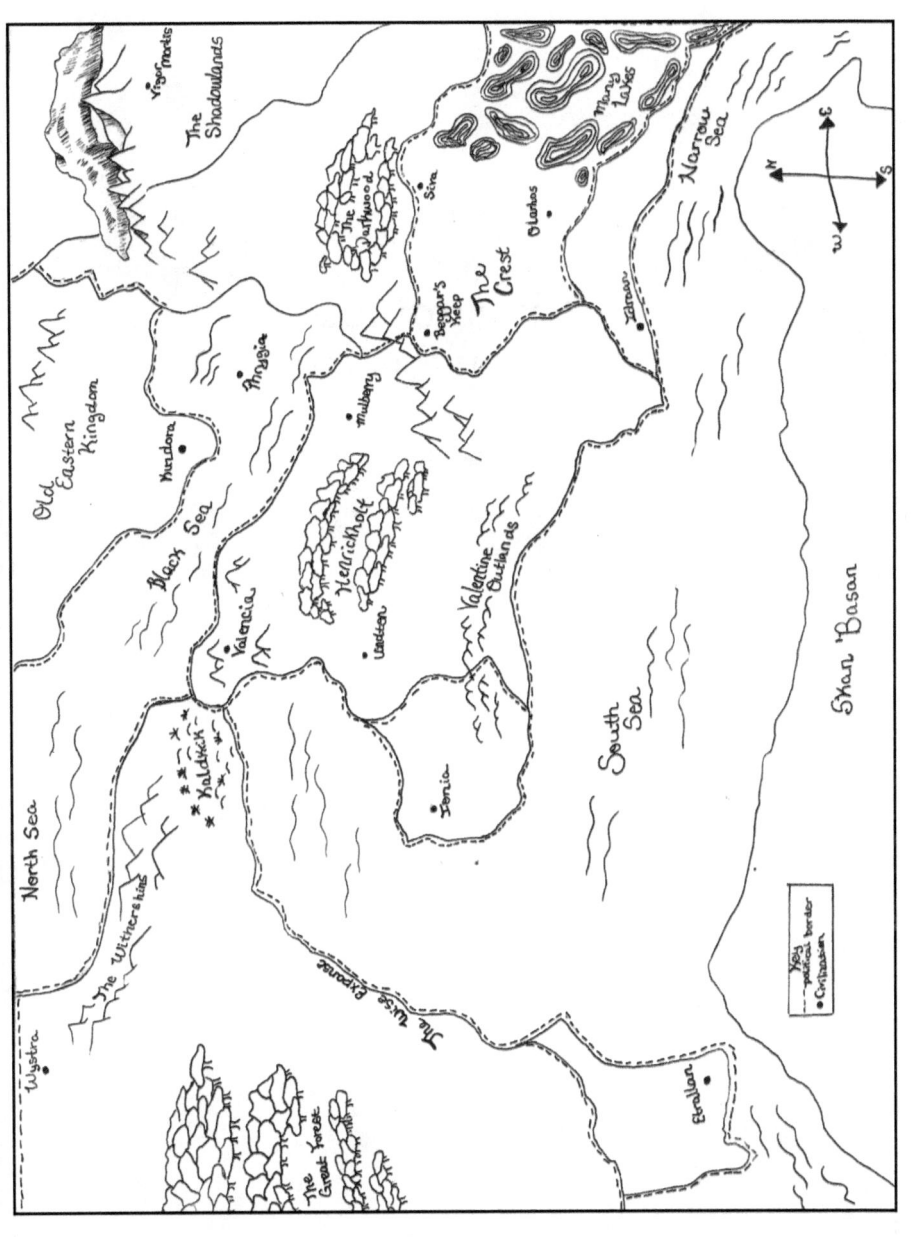

PANDEMONIUM
THE REALM OF THE TORMENTED DEAD.

Prelude:

THE SCARLET CHAIR

Year 398, during the first Wystran rebellion

We made camp in the Kaldkrik, a moldering bog just
beyond the borders of the Golden City. The march was
merciless and brutal; we'd lost three hundred men crossing our
own lands. We knew the risks. We knew the land. We were
tired of the southerners laying claim to our home, weary of
the Valentines telling us how to be—we're Wystrans. We know
how to be. So we assembled and followed the infallible Queen
Collantz over the deadly chain across the Wyse. The motherland
is ours, but her winds care not for whom they cut down. So too,
the swamp mosquitos and blood flies, sucking us dry.

Some of my men gathered round a bonfire, the white smoke
of fresh-fallen pine keeping away the bugs. All was silent aside
from a woman's voice—a Skanu, by her dark skin, and a fighter
by the cords in her forearms. Comely, to be sure, but her eyes
were fierce, not to be trifled with. She wore the leopard-hide
robes of a Keeper; she was a follower of Great Mother Death,
a priestess of Morgana. The men kept their distance as they
listened to her tales with rapt attention.

I sat on a log next to my lieutenant. He was young, only earning his name after my previous lieutenant took a raider's arrow in the neck, not five leagues gone from Wystra. My boy had dragged him to safety best he could, but the damage was done.

"So, what's all this about?" I whispered.

The boy only shrugged. "Some storyteller. Joined the march as we passed through Asvold."

"What's a bloody Skanu doing in a backwater like that?"

"Passing through, I reckon," he said, chewing on a lump of salted venison. "Just like us."

The woman spoke like a poet, her words swaying with subtle rhythm. It was a show, a rehearsed performance. I stretched out my legs and took a swig of watered wine from my skin. Can't be mad at a free show, I thought. Can't be mad at all.

* * *

An excerpt from The Haimiad

Hear my voice, o' blessed spectators, and learn the truth of the Goddess Corrupted! In the Vale Betwixt, she sits upon the Scarlet Chair. Accursed and vain, once liberator—now tyrant—the Lady of the Chair sings her song, breaking the ears of all she surveils. The balance between Life and Death hast shifted, the world off kilter, souls like pebbles sent sprawling in the night.

We are but ants amidst giants, grains of sand in vast oceans.

Hear the tale of the Dread Angel, how she, in her infinite kindness, grew bitter and hateful towards her mortal children. We are nothing but chattel to the Goddess Corrupted, tools to be used and discarded, fuel to feed her gluttonous fires. Hear the tale of Morgana—the Goddess Corrupted, once the ferrier of souls and custodian of the Great Beyond.

She rules the Vale Betwixt, divided by the River Acheron, whose silver waters rise, drowning the earth with preternatural expansion. Once a valley on the brink, now a sea of waste on the edge! The undelivered souls within Morgana suffer and fester, trapped in a place now sequestered by boundless obscura. Careless and lifeless, the angel sits upon her throne, the Chair that Lives, which feasts upon the blood of lives lost and souls sundered.

We are cursed, my friends, cursed to live fitful lives, waking dreams compared to the eternity of torment awaiting us in the underworld. Our benefactor hast fallen, a cruel torturer taking her place, wearing her beloved face. But how could this be? How hast the Gods fallen, descended to pathetic sublimation? How hast Dusk, shepherd of the dead, keeper of souls, fallen so low? Why hast she abandoned us to languish alone?

Yes, friends, I know the tale! Listen closely, and listen well. Hold tight your lovers and children, for they're all you have. Nothing awaits us across the sands. The River Acheron has flooded and congealed—now, a sea of foul intent and festering cruelty. Yes, friends, I know the tale! Listen close, and listen well—for we're all damned to Hell.

* * *

Long ago, in the Vale Betwixt

Baptiste Fournier had begun to fear his lord. Everyone feared his lord, but never the lord's chosen. Never them. For the centuries that Baptiste had spent serving the lord's every whim, overseeing his every errand, Baptiste had known Lord Guilaume Sanguine to be a just and level-headed patron, a man worthy of his immortal station, and of the blood he tithed from his thankless subjects.

Baptiste slouched over his writing desk, rubbing his temples. *Everything good must come to an end.* The philosophers loved the sentiment, but even as a self-styled philosopher, Baptiste spat in the face of impermanence. *What makes a flower so beautiful—its colors? Or the fact that the colors will soon fade?* He once believed all colors were absolute if painted by a master. Now he wondered if the only color standing the test of time was crimson.

Blood. Gods, how Baptiste hated blood! The irony was not lost on him, just as the irony of his bittersweet relationship with philosophy was laid plain to him. Had Baptiste rejected Lord Sanguine's offer all those years ago, he might have died a proud man, an accomplished man. Instead, his high command had declined to the role of a lowly steward in service to a madman, driven wild by centuries of never being denied anything. The lord began his reign over the County of Monrovia as a Stoic, in control of his base desires and primal hungers. But the blood had poisoned him, just as it poisoned everything.

A crow perched on the windowsill and squawked, then pecked at the clouded windows, looking out over a foreign, gray wasteland. Baptiste screamed and hollered at the wretched bird, scaring it back into the dark skies. He had thought living in the Silver Valley might have yielded some relief from the oppression of the mortal world. Instead, it only opened up avenues for the oppression of the immortal one. The lord's chosen could walk by day, lit only by artificial sun and illusory sky, but this boon came at the cost of everything else.

It's that damned throne… Baptiste reflected as he inked his quill, beginning to draft a letter he had put off for far too long. *The chair changed him, I know it has.*

Fleeing the oppression of the sun, Lord Sanguine had led his chosen and his disciples to the Vale Betwixt, following the mouth of the River Acheron where ancient myth foretold of a home for those bound to the night. An eternal throne fit for an undying king. They chanced upon the great keep, waiting unclaimed atop the highest peak overlooking the valley. It was built entirely of limestone and tall like the jagged peaks of the far north. Stained glass windows depicting angelic figures adorned the keep's gray walls. Back then, the long grasses surrounding the site were a vibrant phthalo, and the river shone silver. Now, everything took on the sickly pallor of slate.

"How could such a place lie empty?" asked one of the Chosen when they first explored the keep's expansive walls.

Baptiste had known the answer—rather, he thought he had known. "The Lord was chosen to rule. This is fate, this place was built for us."

And perhaps it was fate that had led them there, but the keep had been built for a purpose beyond his comprehension. A cruel, unforeseen machination led Lord Sanguine to the throne room, so he may lay eyes upon a petinaed chair, with a glowing ruby embedded in its backrest. That chair became the lord's singular obsession every day hence. The lord named it *The Scarlet Chair,* not for its physical features but for the invigoration it seemed to inject into him each time he enjoyed its cushionless seat.

Gone were the days of blood tithes. The lord had his sustenance forevermore. If only such things were so simple. Baptiste should have known better. The fact he failed to detect and dispel such a blatant curse served ill omen to the consequences of his blind admiration for a fallible, imperfect man. Immortal or no, the lord was only a man.

Baptiste had failed his lord and was now reduced to sprawling out on his desk, screaming obscenities at birds through the window.

Dear honored friend, his letter began. He offered no other salutation, nor possessed any hope of it being delivered. Baptiste gambled on the possibility that simply putting his thoughts onto the page might conjure the result he was after. *I write to you because the balance has been broken. I see it now, my misguided nature, my misplaced faith in a false idol. I plead for your forgiveness, to return us to our natural fates and restore all that we've pillaged.* Not a letter, in truth, but a prayer.

When he finished writing, he burned the parchment in his fireplace. As the last corner smoldered, storm clouds gathered over the keep, and mist rolled through the grounds. Rain drummed on the roof, and Baptiste realized his prayer had been answered.

What have I done?

* * *

An excerpt from The Haimiad

No one knows who forged the Scarlet Chair. Likewise, no one could see the veins plunging into the ground, sweeping across the battered valley, wherein runs the River Acheron. Pulsing invisibly, near inaudibly, the Chair siphons the soul's blood from all within its reach.

Hear my voice, o'blessed spectators, know that the ancients wept the day Sanguine discovered his throne's crimson allure! Lo, the gods were powerless to resist his desire, and likewise, the strength the world's blood afforded him. They could not intrude upon his demesne—not lest they be invited.

Addicted to the sweet taste offered by the Chair, the Lord Sanguine launched a campaign herding subjects to his newly established county on the borders between life and death. The blessed valley fell ill as the living quarried her body and cut her hair to build their houses and their temples and their banks. People from near and far flocked to the great County of Monrovia, free from the grip of the Empire, to be ruled instead by a beloved immortal lord.

Yes, dear friends, the people of Monrovia knew Lord Sanguine for what he was. He did not hide his nature, but had promised an end to the wretched blood tithes of generations past—for no one understood that they paid a far steeper price by living within the Scarlet Chair's influence. All was well for a time; the people were fed and wealthy, comfortable and content, until the time came when the gluttonous lord was not.

* * *

Long ago, in the Vale Betwixt

Lightning flashed, thunder clapped. The valley's soil congealed into mud. Baptiste watched the flames in the fireplace dwindle, reflecting on all that had gone so horribly wrong. Three hundred and fifty-two years he had served the good Lord Sanguine. Three hundred and fifty-two years since Baptiste had imbibed the blood of his progenitor. The people in the old kingdom were happy—wary of the blood tithe, as they should have been, but content with the lord's rule. They trusted in the stability of a ruler who could never falter, never to be replaced by a tyrannical son, nor ousted by nefarious factions. Yet Sanguine's court had left the old kingdom in an act of hubris. The old kingdom was good—secure, and fair. Monrovia had started that way, too. But slowly, the lord fragmented before Baptiste's very eyes.

And the day his worldview upended was forever burned in Baptiste's memory. The day he recognized the Scarlet Chair for the curse that it was.

On that wretched day, Baptiste finally realized the fallibility of the infallible, the impermanence of the immortal. A simple act, a declaration in court; nothing sickening nor dramatic, but thoughtless in a way completely out of character for the good lord.

A young woman pleaded divorce from her drunken husband, begged the lord to revoke the father's parental rights to their children. Baptiste watched the lord's empty expression as the woman passionately presented her case, pondered the lord's unhearing ears as she described the manner of monster she was bound to.

With a flick of the wrist, Lord Sanguine decreed the man be sentenced to a life of servitude in the quarry—and that the children become the wards of a banker. He then sent the poor woman away, sentencing her to a life of isolation without a second thought.

Quietly, only after the court was vacant, Baptiste had leaned in and whispered: "My lord, was it necessary to strip the woman of her scions? Surely she is still fit—"

The lord backhanded him without another word. And that was that.

Cracks appeared in the shell and threatened to burst apart. Things only grew worse—the lord acted erratically, screaming at servants and advisers alike, muttering incomprehensibly under his breath when he thought no one was watching. He took pleasure in imparting brutal sentences for minor crimes. That was when executions became a weekly affair—and then a daily one. Soon, though Baptiste was unsure if it was the Chair's doing, a plague ravaged the people of Monrovia, consuming the masses with waves of living necrosis and entropy carried on the backs of rats.

An angel manifested in his study, draping his entire height with an eldritch shadow. Baptiste fell to his knees before the Goddess he had forsaken in his pursuit of power—his hubris. He wept shamefully, pressing his unworthy cheeks to the cold floor. "Please, Great Mother… cleanse this place of the corruption we've sown! We have rebuked you too long! Please… my people are suffering."

Where he expected wrath, Baptiste felt only warmth. Acceptance. He looked up, beheld a face thrown of perfect porcelain, eyes etched of impossible obsidian. The angel wore blackened iron armor, pitted and notched with age, and too heavy for a mortal to wear practically. Her raven's wings folded around them in a tender embrace.

She is here… Dusk has answered my prayer. We are saved…

"You invited me into your house," said she with the myriad voices of a gentle chorus. "Will you accept me again in your heart?"

"Yes! Of course! Anything to put an end to this madness…"

"Look into my eyes!" A sourceless gust invaded the room, ousting the meager fire. "Swear to me you will forsake your bloodlust and adopt again the natural cycle."

Baptiste had grown tired of his unending life, his restless eternity. Unceasing hunger plagued him, insatiable desire ruled him—that, and more, had been the price of his power. Part of him remained reluctant to embrace the Great Mother Death, even after stealing so much time beyond his natural end. *When the lord falls, so do we all. I've summoned death upon my kin.*

"I swear, Great Mother," Baptiste said, venturing to gaze upon those unknowable eyes. "I forsake Sanguine's gift. I will return to you when next you call."

* * *

An excerpt from The Haimiad

Dusk answered the pleading call of Sanguine's betrayer! Invited into the one house for which she held no key, the Great Mother Death melted into the walls seeking the heart of corruption poisoning the Silver Valley.

See, o'blessed spectators, the Goddess was blinded by divine wrath, consumed by a vengeance she dreamed of enacting upon the only one who succeeded at desecrating her holy domain. Before Sanguine dammed the River Acheron, Dusk ferried lost souls to their final rest. Since his accursed occupation, alternate and treacherous routes had been laid to maintain the cycle.

Whether the Lord Sanguine meant to or no, he had disrupted the natural order with his undying presence, and in his ignorance, he unleashed pestilence upon the people he once loved! For these crimes, the Great Mother Death descended upon him in the night, towering over the lord cowering behind his beloved throne.

"Relinquish your perversion and know mercy," decreed the goddess.

The Lord Sanguine did not answer. He was powerless to the will of his seat. Dusk drew her ebon blade, ablaze with holy flames, poised to strike him down in his obstinance, poised to reclaim his foul soul. Her intent to scour the Vampyre from reality, unbeknownst to the goddess, was folly—for the Chair had already laid claim upon the Lord Sanguine, had already devoured his soul.

* * *

Long ago, in the Vale Betwixt

Baptiste watched the Goddess slay his patron from the shadows cast by the light of her holy longsword. He watched with tears in his eyes as the man he had so admired fell at last in the wake of his own conceit. *This is of your own making, my friend. We never should have cheated Death.*

The Lord Sanguine did not resist as the Goddess plunged her blade, simmering into his gut. The mad, aloof expression on his face did not falter, nor did he seem to recognize what had just happened to him. With the brutality of an enraged berserker, Dusk kicked Sanguine to the floor. The once-great lord slumped unceremoniously at the foot of the Scarlet Chair. By all accounts of his condition, Baptiste knew that the death of his progenitor should mean his death, and that of all the vampyres Sanguine had sired.

But death had once again eluded Baptiste Fournier.

Baptiste looked at his tremulous hands, searching for any sign of discomfort or pain. He found nothing of the sort. When he gazed again upon the angel, he saw she was as dismayed as he. He had never witnessed a sight more disturbing. *Gods in hell and up above—what the fuck is happening?*

Dusk staggered back as Sanguine's corpse suddenly ignited, reduced to naught but a pile of ash in an instant. A pulse like heartbeat resounded through the ground, the walls shuddered, and the windows swayed. Dusk reached out to the ashes for the soul that had somehow escaped her grasp.

"No!" Baptiste cried, but he was too late.

The Goddess had laid her hand upon the Scarlet Chair. A pall fell over her porcelain face, a glaze seeped over her obsidian eyes....

And the Goddess Corrupted took her rightful seat on her new throne.

* * *

Year 398, during the first Wystran rebellion

We sat silent as the woman finished her tale. Usually, the bards and poets we encountered on the road had a way of uplifting my men. I marveled at how this storyteller shattered the wills of a hundred men without even a single spell cast. A few boys began arguing about the legitimacy of it—the story was not Wystran by any stretch, that much was clear.

It was borderline heresy to my ears. I've prayed to Morgana on the eve of every battle I've fought. I thought of all the family and friends I'd lost over the years, the soldiers I lost just in the last season crossing the tundra. I shivered to think the Great Mother wasn't waiting for them at the other end.

When most of my boys wandered off, I confronted the Skanu woman. "Why in the name of all that's good would ya tell a story like that? You know where we're headed!"

The storyteller smiled, showing perfect, unnatural ivory teeth. "It is the kindest story I know, Captain."

"If that's the case, I think you'd best move on to another camp."

"No matter—I did not offer my words for succour."

Nothing wears at me like people speaking in riddles. I shook my head. "So you burdened us with doubt for the fun of it? We march with Queen Collantz against the whole of Valencia on the morrow, and my boys are already defeated by your lies!"

The storyteller laughed, reached into her robe, and produced a gnarled twig. She pressed it into my hand, closed my fingers round it. Holding my hand shut, she said: "My story is old, the conflict long resolved—your comrades will know the soul's rest when their time comes. Still, the past exists so that we may comprehend the present and prepare for the future. Think about my words, then think about your quest, eh?"

With that, the woman left, disappearing into the fog.

I thought maybe she was a sorceress or a witch, or more likely, some soothsayer, foreseeing the cloud of lives to be stolen from either side in the days to come and doing what she could to prevent it.

I rolled the twig between my fingers, ruminating on what she had said, the story she had told. I thought about my queen and the brutal path lying before my kin. I'd been a soldier my whole life, and for the first time since leaving home, I thought about turning around to brave the elements of the Wyse. That, I thought, might be preferable to what was to come.

ONE

Tonight, we have lost our god!
I asked my sister where the god went,
And she did not know.
"Poof!" she said, "Gone in a cloud of smoke!"

And I asked, "What of dearest grandmother?
What of her?"
But sister only shrugged.
"We are alone now," she said,
"No one helms the ferry."

The river has flooded with silver
And no one helms the ferry.
We are alone now.

And so I left my home
In desperate search for my god.
But still, I did not find her.
I found only gray carrion fields,
Glowing red by brutal light of day.

The angels have left us,
And I am afraid.
I am afraid we will remain,
So wholly and completely alone.

Saladin (b. -22, death unknown).
"We Are Alone," published Year 12.

I

From the collected journals of a mad wizard

The black doors to Morgana's court stood at the end of a bridge spanning the length of the Screaming Fields. Inside the keep, looming on the highest peak of the Vale Betwixt, the Goddess Corrupted sat upon her accursed throne, the Scarlet Chair, which has remained in the keep's throne room long before she laid claim to it. In her infinite glory, the Goddess watched over her people, those damned to eternal suffering—not because of the weight of their sins, but because they were given no other choice.

The Goddess Corrupted no longer adjudicates—not since the day she first sat upon the Chair.

Standing before her threshold, I felt that pulse I had only before known in dreams, an alien pervasion poisoning the land and the soil. It was I, dear reader, who entered those halls as herald of the Dread Angel's doom. I should tell you I did not make this trek half-heartedly. I should tell you I was anything but fearless. The majesty of the Goddess Corrupted is one of overwhelming splendor. Her visage might rot the eyes of a mortal man; surely it might have meant my own blindness, were I not already afflicted.

I came to her court as a messenger. I sought only to deliver tidings and fair warning. My missive was not one to be taken lightly, but I did not expect the Goddess to pay heed to my words. All for the better, I say—my mission was a gamble, and

if my words had carried weight, likely I would be writing a
different tale altogether.

Do not be fooled; I did not seek out the Dread Angel out
of piety or a sense of duty. I made the dire journey out of self-
interest and simple curiosity.

Morgana did not move from her throne as I approached.
Nor did it offend her as I pulled a handkerchief to wipe my
nose. Weary from travel, I leaned on my staff to catch my
breath and to work up the courage to address the custodian of
life and death.

Redolent air wafted from the kitchens, distinct notes of
turmeric and sage suffusing the room, reminding me of home—
such a strange sensation to feel anywhere in Pandemonium, in
hell. Beneath the comforting aroma, however, lurked the musty
stench of rot and decay. I was in the realm of the damned,
after all, and I was wary she might seek to add my soul to her
collection.

I cleared my throat, squeezing the last reluctant drops from
the bladder at my side to quench my aching thirst. I knew her
patience wore thin, so I raised my arms with joyous incantation.
There is no pleasure equal to reciting one's dreams, even under
duress.

"Dear Lady of the Chair, queen of my heart and ruler of my
soul, I tell you I have seen your ruin. And it fast approaches. He
walks towards you step by determined step, and his heart holds
nothing but finality."

A knight moved to draw his sword, denoted by the scrape
of steel against wooden scabbard. Morgana must have stayed his
blade, for no fatal blow befell me.

"My Chosen has fallen—he has no heart," Morgana
said, her voice the plucking of a harp, a gentle melody with
discordant undertones. "You are misguided, oneiromancer."

"Nay!" Again I heard the vain drawing of blades, and still
no fatal blow was struck.

You see, dear reader, only one such as I can hope to speak against the divine and dare to survive. Reputation—and infamy—are a wizard's steel, temperance against all but the most visceral of intents. "Clouds roil over the horizon east. Your maelstrom rages on, storms plague the sea you have risen, and still he walks on, ascending the Great Stair as we speak! Unrelenting! Monstrous! I've seen him in my dreams; his path is lighted by Dawn's holy rays, rescinding the umbrous black suffocating you all!"

"You've seen his face?" Morgana rose from her seat. The ground pulsed. *Thump, thump.*

"Aye, fair Lady of the Chair, Goddess of my heart... I have. Through swirling desolation, I witnessed his emergence from the black soil of Dysmorphia. I've heard the steady beat of a youthful heart. He strides undeterred, joined by a thousand voices calling for your downfall."

Whispers snaked through the hall. Surely, her courtiers already plotted amongst themselves, unraveling my words for signposts pointing to their selfish gains. Even in death, dear reader, humanity's greed never ceases.

"His sentence has been served; his penance satisfied. He has grown tired of inflicting pain, weary of neglecting his own. Your chosen marches to right the countless wrongs he committed in your name—in life and in death.

"I've seen his mind, experienced his memories. I know his heart, and he will make the world whole again, as you failed to do all those years ago, my Goddess! He will again part the living from the dead, drain the sea, and reclaim the vale so that our souls may once again find peace!"

Morgana unfurled her ebon feathered wings, unleashing a gale that nearly sent me sprawling on my back. Her audience rippled, knights fell reverently to their knees in a cascade of poleyns snapping to the marble floor. Morgana laughed, her voice displacing the air with a solid wall of sound. A hellish stench of sulfur permeated the narthex, the ground heating to burn my feet through my ragged soles.

"Let him come!" Morgana cried, her words resounding through my very being, echoing in my mind. The words that followed would haunt my nightmares for years to come. "I will thrust upon him the weight of worlds; my Chosen will be broken, sundered from the annals of creation!"

The broiling heat subsided, pleasant herbal scents returning in the wake of sulfur's flight. No one dared speak, or even breathe.

I felt Morgana's eyes enrapture my form.

"I will devour him."

II

On the docks of Monrovia

The Vale Betwixt, first layer of Pandemonium

Working the docks was probably the worst job in the whole bloody town. Hours spent toiling in ceaseless hail and rain, suppurating muck bulging between floor planks; truly, there was no greater hell in the whole of the underworld than dock duty. Somehow, Kateryna's name had turned up in the bowl, time and time again. She stopped arguing the results after a month. A year or more had gone by—she guessed, it was hard to tell—since she bothered to attend the drawings.

Kateryna stood vigil in the downpour, watching for stalking serpents or sharks. Such creatures rarely surfaced to feed, but they appeared often enough to warrant a steady stream of begrudging, and unpaid, employment. You would think so many months on dock duty might mean you would grow accustomed to it. But Kateryna never got used to the nauseating sway of the pilings, holding the town above the encroaching waves by a razor's edge.

Behind her, Fulcrum gibbered as he tacked on the welds to the new extensions—a task requiring equal parts ingenuity and madness. Parts of the town were beginning to flood when the old coot arrived from thin air; the other welder had not the reserves of potential to keep up spells to match the demand, and then he succumbed to the pestilence. Fulcrum's sudden appearance, his earnest request to work as the new welder, was something of a miracle.

The old man perplexed Kateryna. He seemed to enjoy his twisted existence beneath Morgana's eternal watch. *Who knows how terrible things are down below... Maybe this is as good as it gets.*

"The storms are getting worse..." Kateryna mused, pulling her hood tight to her face as the rain fell harder. "How far has the level risen since last month?"

"Two meters, give or take," Fulcrum called over his shoulder, hunched over an access hatch. He held a gnarled wand hewn from the branch of a sycamore. The veins in his hand bulged from the immense current of sorcery needed to complete the repair. "Ain't no matter. I crave a challenge!"

A sodden belfry shifted above them; its rotting frame squealed against the weight of a bronze bell, tolling as if to punctuate Fulcrum's insanity.

"There she is!" Fulcrum cackled. "And now we lift her up..." The old man rose, and Kateryna helped him pull on a rope connected to a series of pulleys. The thin cords in his arms rippled as they lifted the southwestern corner of the city block half a millimeter or so. "On to the next one, lass! Lest the waters gain on us!"

Kateryna felt a faint tremor as Fulcrum gathered up his tools; she peered off the ledge to see only brown and black waves rolling beneath the town. Once, the seawater had been somewhat clean, almost drinkable, if boiled for several hours. That had only lasted a little while—now, they collected and boiled rainwater, which always carried a faint aftertaste of spoiled eggs. She took a deep breath and shivered at the stench of decay and congealed shit. There was no escape from that malodor—it was the stench of hell, of Pandemonium.

Another tremor. A skittering sense of panic crawled from the boards to her feet, up her legs. Taking her harpoon, she scanned the horizon for any sign of surfacing serpents. She knew the signs; one had to be drawing near.

"It's the platform settling!" Fulcrum shouted over roaring thunder. "Fifteen months I've been at this, and only a handful of critters come lookin' for snacks!"

Fifteen months? He only just arrived...

She ignored him. He was mad. Obviously, mad.

Then she felt another rumbling—erratic footfalls, something running towards them. She turned and saw a hunched figure lumbering round the belfry. Kateryna dropped the harpoon and ran to the figure.

"Isshiah!"

Isshiah fell into her arms, coughing violently. He was frail, not even fifteen when he first died. Searing boils covered him, weeping pus onto Kateryna's leathers. She gripped his tremulous hand, feeling his flesh burst beneath her touch. *I just saw him yesterday... How could this happen so quickly?*

Kateryna yelled for Fulcrum, but he was gone, already welding the next piling.

Isshiah convulsed in her arms, froth bubbling between his cracked lips. She stroked his dark, matted hair. "Where's your brother, Isshiah? Where's Seth?"

He tried to speak, but he could only wretch, choking on his spit.

Kateryna's calves itched as she felt the third tremor. *Gods, why all at once!* Something stirred below; she knew it.

Someone rang the bell, and a chorus of metallic chants summoned the townsfolk to gather at the quay. A crash of thunder followed by an avian caw—Morgana's Chosen had just arrived with the week's rations. *Perhaps... just this once, he'll listen.*

Slinging Isshiah over her shoulder, Kateryna made for the quay, pushing through disgruntled, starving onlookers.

Black wings unfurled before gray clouds, and the rains reduced to a mere drizzle as Morgana's Chosen descended on the back of his griffin. The beast landed weightlessly, and the crowd closed in around it.

The rider's sabatons crunched in the sand as he dismounted. Morgana's Chosen stood a head taller than the tallest Monrovian, his hulking shadow casting a dire pall over the pleading villagers. Kateryna bared her teeth, shoving past her neighbors with as much speed and vigor as she could muster.

"Only twenty today," said Morgana's Chosen, his voice devoid of sympathy. "Pull your numbers."

"Cain!" Kateryna howled over their protesting cries, but the rider did not hear—she was surrounded by a screaming, cursing mass only concerned for its next meal.

"Damn you, demon!" yelled the man next to her.

"You're killing us all!" declared an old woman.

Her every step was marked by a new curse cast upon the gray man wearing the black armor of the Chosen. They cursed the rider to the depths as they begged for his meager gifts. Yet it was Kateryna who stood before him, buckling beneath the weight of a friend, pleading for someone else's life. It was Kateryna who called the man by name, rather than the titles bestowed upon him.

"Cain, please!"

Finally, the rider turned. Empty black eyes fell on her, then traveled to the unconscious boy on her shoulders. Wordless, the rider approached and offered a hand to help ease Isshiah to the ground. The mob's protest fell silent as they backed away to give the dying boy air.

"Help him…" Kateryna said, weeping. "For the love of all that's good, you can't let his soul fall into the depths."

"He's beyond help," said Morgana's Chosen. "His blood is tainted."

"No… he was fine just last night…" *I swear I just checked on him.*

The rider unsheathed his dagger, the blade glimmering under the lantern light. Without ceremony or even bare warning, he slit Isshiah's throat, tenderly shutting the boy's eyes.

The mob exploded with outrage, though they gave the dangerous armored man a wide berth. From a safe distance, they screamed and yelled and cursed—but they were powerless to resist the Dread Angel's will.

"Scourge!"

"You sick bastard!"

Kateryna fell to her knees, eyes locked on Isshiah's fouled blood covering her hands. She knew what would follow the contact—she had experienced it already. *Where might you land, my friend? Could there be somewhere kinder for you to seek succor? Or is this as safe as it gets?*

A subtle, barely perceptible quake of gangplanks called her attention back to the sea. *Perhaps this is a mercy, after all…*

III

From the collected journals of a mad wizard

I was in attendance that morning on the docks, dear reader. I heard the poor boy's flesh tear open, as Morgana's Chosen cut his throat with practiced indifference. Such things do not shock one as wizened as I—not anymore.

Know that the boy did not die that day. Not in the way you will die, one day, now that everything's been settled. No, his soul was simply transposed, ousted from one vessel to search for another.

This is the reality of the underworld, what it means to suffer in Pandemonium.

The rider wiped his dagger clean on the boy's trousers, sliding it back into the scabbard on the small of his back. His movements were calm and deliberate, emotionless. The rider's job was to keep the Monrovians alive and obedient—the diseased boy was merely a threat to those ends.

Disposing of a plague carrier did well to keep the Monrovians alive, but did little to ensure their obedience. The mob erupted in a cacophony of fervent protest. Drawn from my work by the ensuing chaos, I was swept up in a tide of bodies, where I was incessantly nudged and bumped, shoved this way and that.

I nearly slipped on a river stone. A man caught me, then picked up the stone, testing its weight in his hands.

I put a hand on his shoulder, whispered: "If he killed the boy without remorse, do you think he would spare a second thought for a stone thrower?" I grinned as I heard the stone plop back into the sewage at our feet.

The rider's steed let out a strident squawk and spread its wings, rearing on its hind legs before stamping its taloned feet hard onto the planks. That shut up the whole lot. Bred by Morgana herself, griffins have a natural affinity for scaring the pants off even the most belligerent of people.

With the townspeople back in order, the Chosen unclipped a sack from his saddle—from which came the alluring scent of freshly-baked sourdough.

"Draw your numbers!" he yelled to his matron's subjects.

Utterly disheartened, they shuffled into a single-file line to draw lottery tickets.

When I came to the front, I simply fumbled about like a mindless old git until the rider dismissed me. I have had much success maintaining such facades; I have had years of practice. For you see, dear reader, the greatest illusions are not spells at all....

I listened on from the shadows of an overhanging porch. Twenty numbers were called, and twenty villagers were given bread while a hundred more starved.

After that, it did not take long for them to return to their hovels.

Understand, dear reader, that I was in Monrovia to perform important reconnaissance. For months leading up to my fell expedition, my dreams were plagued by visions of hell—so I made it my duty to go there in person. I had yet to dream of Morgana's Chosen, but in meeting him that day, I realized his significance to my mission. Call it intuition, call it coincidence, if you will—both are great assets to a thoughtful wizard.

"Cain," said a young woman. The speaker was Kateryna, near as tall as he and strong of arm, she was forever tasked with

guarding me as I welded extensions on the pilings. I wondered
who might she be to the Chosen to address such a figure by his
given name. "You could have asked her for help…" she said.
"You didn't even try."

The rider finished packing his saddle before he ventured
a response. "Don't call me that… I am Syr Arthur. You'd best
remember that."

"Mother never called you that. Not once. Neither shall I."

Plates of armor rattled as Syr Arthur Cain pointed to the
sky, to the gentle drizzle that was soon to grow into a torrent.
"The Goddess sees all, Kateryna. I am just as beholden to her
will as you, and everyone else."

"You'll never change," Kateryna said, the knuckles in her
hand popping into place as she tightened her fist. "I don't know
why I try."

Morgana's Chosen saddled his mount and, without a word,
kicked off into the skies beyond the clouds.

Whether it was intuition or coincidence that moved me
to eavesdrop, intuition alone drove me to run to my hovel like
a schoolboy on an errand given by a beloved uncle. Beneath
Kelvin's bridge—made entirely of limestone but enchanted
to be weightless, and thus a welcome addition to the rickety
shantytown—my haunt lay in a crevice between the foundation
of two sagging tenements. Though hardly free of the damp, it
offered me a secure place to lay out my bedroll and enact my
magic undisturbed.

There, I found an early slumber. I weaved the words to call
forth a prophetic dream, to cast my oneiromancy. But I was too
hasty, and I slipped, falling right into the pits of my mind as if I
had been three days starved of sleep.

The nightmare that came to me owed not to fatigue, dear
reader. I tell you, what I saw was dire. We oneiromancers oft
invite our dreams, yet this vision was no benevolent visitor,
knocking gently upon the door to my psyche with tea and
cookies. This was a nightmare in truth—a terror of the greatest

sort. I will not recount exactly what I saw, for it pains me still to think of it.

Instead, I offer a verse. It is as much as I'm willing to share.

Blood on the walls.
A dark path,
Carved through the halls.
A woman lay dead
Sundered and appalled.
There's so much,
Blood on the walls.

Fear not the change in my type's countenance, it was not my hand that moved my pen. Such things are natural symptoms of oneiromancy. Recalling the dreams of others sometimes invites their disembodied will. I had never dreamt through the eyes of a divine, but I did that night, and I hope I never will again.

This is the cost of oneiromancy. Not only does your mind become host to strange forces of the cosmos, but so too your body and soul. Now you know, dear reader.

Now you know.

IV

On the docks of Monrovia

The Vale Betwixt, first layer of Pandemonium

Kateryna sat legs dangling off the edge of the limestone bridge connecting the quay to the tenements. How the damned thing never sank with the town was beyond her, but she was thankful, at least, for a place she could sit on solid ground.

She watched the horizon as the sun dimmed like a lantern burning out. The sun did not set or rise in Pandemonium. It turned on and off; the sun was an illusion cast for some eldritch reason outside her reasoning.

Holding out a shaking hand, still stained with blood and pus—Isshiah's blood and pus—Kateryna wished desperately for a smoke. Something, anything, to grant a modicum of comfort. Such comforts were rare, traded for bread by the occasional drifter searching for a way out of Pandemonium. Myth told of a silver river leading to the waking world, but if something like that existed, it was now buried beneath the sea.

I can't do this… How can this happen again?

The pestilence that had killed the people of Monrovia followed them into the underworld, lurking in the background, so that the anxiety of contracting it again prevented any hope of a restful moment. Kateryna often wondered why she and her neighbors ended up there. The only common thread was that they had all died the same way.

Kateryna let out a sharp laugh just to hear it echo off the waves. She let out another, and the guffaw soared with the wind into the distance. She hoped Morgana heard her—saw Kateryna laughing at the Dread Angel's pathetic hubris. *Strike me down, oh glorious benefactor. Spare me the pain of my second death!*

She spat thick bile into the waters below, her waste dissolving to join countless others. The roiling muck inched closer every day, faster than they could lift, even with Fulcrum's obsessive labors. If not pestilence, then festering floods. If not one death, then another. And so on, and so forth, for the rest of eternity. *That's how it goes, isn't it?* That was how the holy books described it, anyhow.

Overcome by a fit of laughter, Kateryna doubled over with uncontrollable despair. She rolled on the ground and pounded her fists on the bricks, hitting hard so her callused skin tore open, so she could feel something other than illness and regret.

"I heard what happened," a man said behind her. Embarrassed, Kateryna pulled herself to her feet, swinging about to face Isshiah's elder brother.

"Seth," she said. "I'm sick."

Seth shook his head. "Me too."

"Have you… gone through this before?"

"We all have—that ain't a mystery."

"Right, but you—"

"I had it."

"Okay."

Seth grunted, his face etched in stone, his demeanor just as cold. Talking with him was always difficult. Kateryna could never understand why. She knew she had known him in life, but the specifics were lost to the fog.

I've hurt you. So bad, and yet I don't think either of us knows how… We just know that I did.

"I begged Cain to help."

"Little good that could do... but thanks for trying." Seth looked down at his bare feet, dirty and torn. "Isshiah was as good as dead by the time he found you. He declined fast. So will we."

Kateryna did not know what to say—she just looked into his eyes, searching for what she had once found there, long ago. There was nothing but iron.

"I'm going after him," Seth said. It was not up for debate; his mind was made up. Somehow, she could tell that by his tone of voice, the flattening of his lips.

"That's insane," she said. "Even if you managed to get a skiff to shore, you'd be eviscerated by whatever beasts hunt in the fields."

"One step closer, then. He's just a kid, Kat. I can't leave him to do this all alone. I am dying anyway, so what does it matter?"

It did matter. It mattered a lot. The thought of him going out all alone made her sick to her stomach. "I guess there's something to that."

Seth fumbled in his pockets, pulled out a cigar wrapped with a thick tobacco leaf. "I got this a while back. Last time someone made the trip here. I meant to give it to you." He handed it to her. "Keep it dry, eh?"

Kateryna smoked alone well into the night, trying to see the blocked pathways that made her gut churn with worry at the thought of Seth and Isshiah in danger—out of her reach.

When the cigar was spent, and Kateryna could no longer abide the wind and the rain, she returned to her mother's house. She had torn up her hood so she could wrap her face and hands like a leper.

Her mother stood in the dim candlelight of the kitchen, waiting as she always did, her mouth curling into a mournful smile when their eyes met.

"Stay away… I don't want you to—"

But her mother had already swept her up, holding her just as she had when Kateryna was a little girl. Kateryna tried to wriggle free, to spare her mother the fatal contact with the sores already blossoming on her hands and face, but a mother's love transcends such things, and soon she gave in to the embrace. And she savored it, knowing such comforts were soon to be forever lost.

"Thank you…."

V

From the collected journals of a mad wizard

Leaving my nightmare, my dreams shifted to follow Syr Arthur Cain for the first time. Normally, when I dream, I stand in the subject's shoes, seeing through their eyes and experiencing their thoughts. But not Morgana's Chosen— for his heart was buried far away, claimed by the Goddess Corrupted. I followed him from a bird's-eye view, and I felt only echoes of his pathos.

Cain stood atop a mountain peak, reduced to a mere island in the swath of the congealed sea overflowing the Vale Betwixt. The dimming sun shone through parting clouds, and the surveilling rains dwindled again to a drizzle before ceasing entirely. Such peace is a rarity in Morgana's demesne, but even the eyes of a divine are not infinite when she has extended her will upon unnatural domains. In the clarity of the moment, Cain felt a weight lift from him as the sun's illusory glow melted away, painting the sky with a wash of baby blue and pastel pink.

He scratched the chin of his trusted companion, the griffin bestowed upon him by Morgana, created in the aspect of a raven after the Dread Angel's own visage. Such gifts were reserved only for Her Chosen—and gifts were not given freely in Morgana's court.

Not one for sentiment, Cain did not name the beast. While the Monrovian fog blocked his understanding of this feeling, I later learned he had lost a number of horses in his life—during the crusades to quell the Kaza'duran invasion. Imagine his surprise when the magnificent griffin-foal told him its chosen name. *Montauk,* she called herself, the words written directly into Cain's mind.

Temporarily free of his mental imprisonment, Cain swung his leg over Montauk's muscular torso and commanded her back into the skies, away from the Dread Angel's keep. The rare moments of clear weather marked the only times he dared resist his matron's will. Cain was claimed—that was laid bare—but without eyes to watch his every move, he was free to do as he wished.

He leaned forward in the saddle, gripping the horn. Wordlessly, he bid Montauk be swift, and the griffin beat her great wings, then dove into an updraft carrying them far above the clouds where the air was thin and the burden light. It did not take long to reach the sorry town. The horizon swelled with moldering wood structures hanging by ropes and rusted cables. The people there lived on the razor's edge—including his family, whom he had neglected time and time again.

Montauk landed in a hidden crevice between intersecting rooftops; a poorly kept secret, for you can hide nothing from a probing oneiromancer, nor from curious children with nothing better to do than to climb the bloated structures. Cain dropped from the wall and walked a familiar path. Up six flights of creaking stairs, down three, a left turn, up two more. He knocked gently on the door at the end of the gantlet, hanging crooked in its frame. Through the gaps, he saw candlelight flickering, swift movement accompanied by measured footsteps.

Anastasia opened the door.

Cain's breath caught in his throat as if it were the first time he was looking into her icy blue eyes. Each time he laid eyes on her, followed the path of subtle curves through her nightgown, he was beset by a barrage of ancient memories, long withheld. His wife was the only person capable of competing with the Dread Angel's hold on him—but such episodes of lucidity were fleeting, for she did not hold his heart.

"Kat has fallen ill," Anastasia said.

Cain looked at his boots. "I'm sorry."

"I know." Droplets of condensation dripped from the roof's edge, drumming into rain pots. Monrovia sang a slow, lamenting refrain. Anastasia caressed Cain's scarred cheek with a callused hand, reclaiming his attention. "You can ask her. Just this once."

"I cannot," he croaked, shaking his head. "I cannot."

She dropped her hand, faded back into the house, the door hanging ajar. "I know."

Thunder rolled in the distance. The storms would soon begin again. Cain almost turned around.

"Will you stay awhile?" Anastasia asked. "It's been so long since your last visit."

"Until the storm sets in"

She nodded.

Cain stepped gingerly into the entryway. His weight and dirty armored boots made the planks squeal regardless of his intention. One of the bedroom doors was sealed—he heard his daughter's muffled sobs through the walls and knew her pain was his doing.

Anastasia led him back to her bedroom—a place they never shared, not really—and helped him to doff his armor. Naked, he sat on the floor while she bathed him with a damp rag, wiping away dirt and blood with every stroke. He loved her— how could he keep forgetting he loved her? His wife. His world. She regarded him as if he had done no wrong. Always forgiving, always waiting with open arms. Always receiving nothing in return.

Cain stared at the wall, wishing he could remember what her intimate touch felt like. Just being there with her was a risk; each time his memory returned, he vowed never to risk lying with her again, for the consequences were too dire. His matron's wrath knew no bounds, and her envy was all the more encompassing.

His wife circled in front of him, sat across him, simply to absorb his eyes in hers. She saw him for what he was, knew the blood on his hands; she had washed it away time and time again. She held him anyway, savored the fleeting moments between storms. Her love must have spanned the horizon, so too her compassion.

Together they stood. Anastasia removed her nightgown, and Cain stared at her thin form, engraving every detail into memory. She had always been thin, malnourished, even in life, and so he had always worried for her health. But it was chronic illness, back then, fending off the padding of the hard-fought luxury he had won for his family. The malady made short work of her compromised body.

And that.... was all on Cain's shoulders.

She invited him to her bed, where they lay skin-to-skin, warming one another until sticky sweat clung to them. And still she held him, and he her.

That night, marked by the rarest comfort known to him, Cain made the mistake of falling asleep, lulled to dreams by those percussive pots. He failed to notice the refrain swelling into chorus.

You already know the horror to which he awoke.

VI

You were only a boy. You were not to blame. Not then, not yet. So young, so impressionable, when Dusk first came to you and offered her love. How were you to know the price you'd pay? You never thought love would find you, and so you jumped at the first opportunity to find it yourself.

Do you remember that feeling you had when you heard your father's boots pad up the deck? That skip and subsequent sinking. The excitement for his return after being absent for weeks at a time. Do you remember the acrid aroma of dirt and soot that followed him wherever he went?

On the nights he was given leave to return home, you begged him for stories. But he'd only scratch his overgrown beard thoughtfully, and say he had not much to tell. Your father was no storyteller. Not that father, at least.

I am. So, listen closely.

Sometimes your mother swept into the room, on those rare occasions they were dismissed on the same night. She seemed to float to him, as if pulled by gravity towards him. You used to think nothing could keep them apart. Grasping his face, covered in coal dust, she pressed her lips to his.

Such moments were the only time you remember seeing him smile.

Often, that gentle exchange was all the tenderness they could afford. Other times, when your father had more energy and less pain, he'd wrap her in his arms and spin about the room as if they had suddenly been transplanted to a ball at the Governor's manor.

When he dipped her low, pressed the tip of his nose to hers, he whispered so no one else could hear. But you heard—you always heard: "I love you, darling. Like the sun loves the moon."

On a winter evening, just before the solstice, your mother didn't make it home. Such things weren't alarming, but she had sent a letter telling you to expect her back; the governor had fired all his staff. Your father stopped at the threshold, raising his eyebrows as he found you shaking on the porch.

"What is it, boy?"

You shook your head, closing your stinging, puffy eyes. You didn't know why, but you were worried. Beyond worried. *Mother should be home by now.*

The sky was red, and white ash fell like snow. You watched helplessly as your father turned around and, without another word, disappeared into the gloom. You nearly called out, nearly ran behind him to help with whatever fell errand he'd set his mind to. But you didn't. You couldn't. You were just a boy.

Though he never promised his return, his absence over the next few days felt like a cruel introduction to the art of lying through one's teeth.

Soon, you were out of food. The day after, the governor's men came knocking, armed and armored, and something told you to slip out the back door and never look back. You had no one else to guide you, so you trusted your gut.

The ash kept falling—it wouldn't stop for a year or more. You later found out why. By some force of greater sorcery, a desert had spread across the province of Kaldea, toppling the seat of the Empire in an instant. The Great City of Baltaire was no more. The world was off-kilter, and would remain so for the rest of known history.

Though you lived in a nameless colony across the South Sea, your village wasn't spared from the conflict that followed the desert's arrival. The sands brought Idraan, a sandstone fortress replacing the fallen capital, inhabited by otherworldly serpentine creatures that called themselves *Kaza'dur.*

The streets became a warzone. As more soldiers dressed in the Imperial colors fell, the more your fellow orphaned street urchins disappeared in the night. You didn't know they were being sold at pop-up markets in the neighboring settlements, taken by the Kaza'dur.

That was why you ran to the chapel on a hilltop outside of town. The chapel's thick walls had yet to crumble, and it seemed the grounds were untouched by scaled fingers.

You bent the knee to the Lady of Dusk, shepherd of souls, sister to Dawn. You prayed she would see your parents to safety, and you devoted everything from that moment hence to her name. They took you in, made you their own, and for the next several years, they provided sanctuary against the tide of invasion.

A priest called Ibrahim took you under his wing. He adopted you as his child, and you lived with him. When you asked for his family name, he told you he had none. "The only name worth remembering is the name Dusk bestows upon you."

Ibrahim was a slender, meek man; his skin dark, and his nose and ears decorated with silver jewelry. He was Skanu, native to this land your people had conquered and colonized— now, besieged by crueler conquerors, besides. The true people of Skan'basan were a rare sight in the colonies; you had only met a few in your short life. Most had been shipped across the South Sea, or they isolated in the wilderness to escape the sprawling grip of the Empire.

What you'd remember most about Ibrahim was his eyes.

Sharp as a quill, vibrant as a clematis in full bloom, his eyes commanded attention, demanded respect—more so than words could hope to achieve, yet he was made of words. He had taught you the tenants of Zulma, the Great Mother Death, known to you as Dusk. So too, he taught you to read and write and speak with eloquence. "All people should know these things," Ibrahim would say when you grew frustrated by your studies. "Dusk leaves little for the eye, so we must read by what light remains."

After you took communion for the first time—taking a sip of spirits from the skullcap of a long-dead prophet—Ibrahim brought you to a cave in the mountains.

You were waylaid by a unit of Kaza'duran foot soldiers, and laid eyes on their cold, scaly faces for the first time. They had the skin and heads of snakes, each one boasting a different pattern of bright and earthy colors. You felt the indifference in their hearts—the same a man might feel, stumbling upon a dog in the street. Ibrahim convinced them you were his slave, that he was a loyal adopter, and had already bent the knee. They believed him, and you never forgot that even he, this paragon, could lie through his teeth.

When you reached the mouth of the cave, he refused to enter. "You must descend alone, my son." He took your clothes, and you ventured into the black naked, free of burden and devoid of armor. "Listen to the waves, the drops!" he called at your back, just as the last of the sun's light was swallowed by encroaching walls.

You listened… and you heard more in that moment, than in every other moment of your short life combined.

Following the echoing drops of condensation, you came upon a spring, and you bathed in the warm water. A gentle drop splashed on your forehead. A woman sang, her voice resounding through the water and you felt her embrace. She whispered her request; her breath on your ear and neck sent shivers down your spine.

"I will never stop loving…" You promised her.

A light in the water shimmered, and the pool became perfectly temperate to grant you unique comfort, matching your body's needs that even you were not aware of.

"I devote myself to you. Body and soul."

In that moment of tender bliss, you never could have imagined the lifetime of blood that awaited you. Nor could you imagine the furnace of eternal torment sweltering in anticipation of your soul's arrival.

Once, you were alive. Truly alive. Once you were that naive little boy, floating naked in the water, consumed with peace and love, driven to cherish your Goddess's children. Once, you were a person who sought to facilitate life, to nurture it and watch it blossom.

And yet, even you strayed so far, so quickly.

TWO

In our darkest hour
We trudged through the sands.

Beneath clear, open sky
We boiled in our armor.

My horse collapsed at my feet
And I was thankful.

Her suffering was great
Existence tortured.

I did not give her a name
If I had, I would not have remembered.

Unknown author.
"March to Idraan," found on a soldier's body, Year 31.

I

On a thoroughfare in Monrovia

The Vale Betwixt, first layer of Pandemonium

There had been no time to think; she could only run. Kateryna had no desire to think. Thinking meant reflection, and what she had just seen was nothing she wanted to reflect upon. No, instead, she ran across town, surrounded on all sides by mass degradation. Every one of her neighbors was beset with pestilence in an instant.

Morgana's visage was burned in Kateryna's memory; she saw the Dread Angel's sickeningly perfect face every time she blinked, felt her grip constricting her lungs with every breath. *This is my fault.* How could it not be? She had, after all, taunted the Goddess Corrupted in full view of her million eyes. *I called to her—and she answered...*

No time for doubts, nor second-guessing. Kateryna now had but one goal, and not a second to spare.

I will find you, mother. I swear it.

Sounds of carnage spilled from the adjacent block: blood spraying, limbs splitting apart, bone chilling ululations of the damned as they are sequentially torn to ribbons by their matron. *I am prey. She is saving me for last.*

The warped, old faering she and Fulcrum sailed to tack up welds on the outer stilts was still docked at the pier. Kateryna threw her harpoon on the deck, leapt into the rear seat, and rowed with a fervor she had never known, pumping her arms faster and harder than she thought possible. *I cannot let Morgana have me,* she thought as the sluggish little vessel slogged through the grime collecting on the water's surface. *I must find her!*

Kateryna had seen it through the gaps in the wall panels: the Dread Angel had gingerly opened their front door, as if checking in between errands; light footsteps cascading down the hall, her mother's baleful scream... her death knell.

No! She would not think of it. The burden would only weigh her down. *Her soul is out there, somewhere, and I must be swift.*

* * *

Sailing the Congealed Sea

The Vale Betwixt, first layer of Pandemonium

Viscous water lapped against the side of the faering as she rowed. Heavy, dark droplets fell from the mast, dotting her soaked clothes with dark stains. The storm had subsided to a drizzle. Kateryna wondered if Morgana was tired—if such things were even possible for a divine.

The sun was burning anew for the day, shining bright through meager clouds. Rays warmed her broad shoulders; if Kateryna had been a superstitious person, she might have thought it symbolic—sailing out on a quest against Dusk, with the light of Dawn at her back. But Kateryna had given up on such things. In her tortured prolonged existence, she was certain the gods above did not give a single shit about the souls writhing down below.

She was, like everyone else damned to Pandemonium, forgotten.

The wind picked up, so she lowered the sail and traded oar for tiller. As she cut across the Congealed Sea, she searched for any sign of Seth; he had left a few hours ahead of her, but she was by far the stronger rower. If he lived, she could catch him. Then she might not feel so alone... so discarded.

A nauseating surge rocked the boat, sending it listing starboard. Kateryna pulled at the sails, using every ounce of strength to keep the vessel from capsizing. It settled, and she fell sprawling on the deck, her own wind stolen from her chest.

There's no way... Seth was not a sailor in life, just a hobbyist who seldom took a fishing boat out on Lake Valentine—from what depths this memory resurfaced, Kateryna was unsure. Still, strange thoughts arrived like overdue letters on the doorstep of her mind, the farther away she got from Monrovia. *He can't be alive. There's no way.* She hoped desperately that she was wrong, yet she saw no alternative, and that realization somehow crushed her heart, which had already been stamped flat in the dirt.

Seth was a kind soul, a loyal, loving man. But such traits, as much a boon to his loved ones as to himself, did not make Seth a demigod hero capable of striding the deadly planes of hell.

It did not change the fact that his body was eating itself from the inside out, just like hers.

Every gust, every drop of water, carried with it this taste of fury—of rage. Kateryna wondered if it was her own dissociated emotions manifesting in front of her, but began to doubt that once a raindrop landed in her eye... and she felt envy, the pure, unadulterated, jealous rancor of a spoiled child. *That's not me. That has never been me.*

Hours went by, memories and understanding rolled in. The air was sweet, cool as it traveled down her inflamed windpipe. She scanned the horizon for land, only knowing the shore opposed the sun, or so claimed one of the mad visitors passing through Monrovia.

Another surge sent vibrations through the worn planks of the boat. Ahead, she saw the rotting tail of a serpent whip out of the water before slithering back below. *There it is.* Kateryna retracted the sails, grabbing her harpoon with one hand and the gunwale with the other. *My second death awaits.*

Her stomach lurched as the boat suddenly launched towards the clouds, riding a wave taller than the hobbled belfry at the quay.

Struggling against inertia, Kateryna braced the harpoon against the deck and prepared for impact. It was futile, she knew; they were barely able to fend off such a beast with twenty armed men in the watchtowers. She was but one woman alone on the sea—death was assured. She had known it would happen. So did Seth.

A tangle of bulging cords emerged from the water, encasing the vessel in a cage of entropic scales. Kateryna blinked turgid seafoam from her eyes, opened them to look into the gaping maw of the serpent, lined with countless rows of sword-like fangs, every gap a waterfall. Its breath was a low rumble as the boat slid down toward the serpent's undulating esophagus.

"Spare me no pain!" she screamed at the serpent, sores in her own throat ripping open. "You never have before!"

Kateryna leapt from the deck just as the serpent snapped its jaws, crushing the boat to splinters. She fell, content to watch the translucent surface of the sea rush up towards her at a quarter of the speed it should have. How amusing, that adrenaline should play such a role in the afterlife.

A pulse resounded through the realm, a subtle pull she had grown used to, now obviously out of place so far from Morgana's fog and storms: a tug on her soul, an external hunger, reeling her back in.

Something possessed Kateryna to thrust the harpoon in front of her, then, catching the serpent's throat, which slowed her descent by tearing a ragged rent in the creature's dead flesh. Acrid fluids showered her as she dangled from the harpoon in mid-air.

The serpent screeched a horrific ululation, lashing violently in every direction, jostling Kateryna senseless, her head a pounding, muddled mess of misplaced thoughts and half-forgotten convictions. She had resigned herself again to just let go, to free herself of certain pain in favor of uncertain pain at the other end. She was about to let go—until she saw the rider gliding towards her just over the horizon, the wings of his griffin extended in a wide, all-encompassing arc.

"Cain!"

Again and again, she cried out to him.

A thousand times she had begged him for help. A thousand times he had denied her. She hated the man for abandoning them, for driving her mother mad, for choosing his wicked goddess over his own family. And still she called his name, praying to any who would hear, that this might be the time he finally listened, that he would finally give in to his duty as a father, rather than a god's Chosen.

"Cain!"

The griffin drew closer. She could see the shimmer of its ebon wings billowing in the wind, its yellow slitted eyes narrowing on her. Kateryna looked into her father's empty, black eyes as he flew past her, leaving her to her fate. Her heart broke a third time, seeing on his face the expression of a stranger passing another on the road.

"Cain…"

Shame appeared in place of salvation. She was a fool, in truth. Her head pounded, pressure about to explode. The pain of her straining fingers, gasping lungs, her whip-lashed spine… it was too much, and her grip was failing. She gaped at the roiling waves of brown and black below.

Wherever I end up, she thought in a moment of perfect clarity. *I will be one step closer to finding her.*

Kateryna let go and fell towards the sea.

II

From the collected journals of a mad wizard

I do not expect you to sympathize with Morgana's Chosen, dear reader. He does not deserve it, nor does he need it. He will, however, earn your utmost attention in the pages to come— perhaps, even your respect.

He has earned mine.

Morgana was a vengeful, possessive matron. But she was not always so. During most of Cain's life, and for the millennia leading up to it, Dusk served as the shepherd of the dead, escorting the souls of the dearly departed across the treacherous rapids of the River Acheron.

All of that came to an end around the time the Kaza'dur appeared in our world. That was unprecedented, and even now, centuries later, at the time of my writing, we feel the ripples of their forceful arrival.

Nevertheless, some time after they appeared, Dusk became Morgana—and all hell broke loose.

That night in Monrovia, Morgana left the comfort of her beloved throne and wreaked slaughter en masse upon the poor townspeople. She started with Anastasia, the only soul capable of stealing her most prized possession, and sent her soul careening through the ether with naught but a cold glance. A flick of her wrist spread late-stage pestilence to the rest.

If not for the wards sewn into my tarp, I too would have succumbed to Morgana's plague; my body bloated and scarred with burst pocks and cysts. My soul lost to the void. This is why a wizard must always take ample precautions, dear reader. We are not infallible.

Though I was spared the illness, a terrible fever took me as I dreamt: it began with the nightmare, then my synchronous shadowing of Cain. I twisted and turned, woke briefly for a gulp of water, then I returned to my fitful slumber to find a room painted red with blood, lit solely by the presence of a divine.

Not only would I see through one's eyes that night, but I would also gaze into them.

* * *

Morgana stood a head and a half taller than Cain, who was a hulk of a man in his own right. He sagged broken to his knees, staring at tremulous hands, dyed crimson.

The Dread Angel was horrible in her beauty: paper-white skin, contrasted by lips and eyes black as night. Her face was carved marble, honed to perfect proportions, her figure full and shapely as befit the Mother of Darkness, the Matron of Night. Mounted upon her back were the wings of a great raven, their span so encompassing that she could shroud a room full of people in her dark embrace.

Her inhuman countenance unreadable, she glowered at Cain, who bent before her, kissing the festering floorboards. He cowered like a dog at her heel, mumbling desperate apologies under his breath in an unending loop.

Morgana smiled, summoning illusory compassion, feigning understanding for the folly of a man's heart.

As an outside observer, I saw a twisted kind of satisfaction in that grin, words written in my mind's eye: *Yes, you are mine. Remember, you are mine, not hers. Never hers!*

"Rise," decreed the Goddess Corrupted, her harmonious voice dripping with lascivious allure.

Cain rose. He was splattered head to toe with the remains of his love—his true love.

She smacked him across the face with an open palm, a petty gesture in the hands of one that damned an entire populace without raising a finger.

"Forgive me, dear Lady. I have forgotten myself."

"Yes. You have."

Cain slowly raised his head to meet her gaze. Even to him, a man who had seen them countless times before, the Dread Angel's eyes were gravity wells, pulling in everything that dared to draw near.

"You understand, my dear Chosen," Morgana cooed, "why I demand undying loyalty from you?"

He nodded meekly.

"Because love is finite," she said anyway. "And I require all you have to give. I have granted you my hand. You are mine— and thus, you have nothing else to give."

"Yes, mistress."

"Alas," the goddess sighed, caressing his chin with soft, slender fingers. "It is your nature to stray. To make the same mistakes, time and time again. I have been so very patient with you, my love."

"Yes. More than I deserve…"

"I cannot forgive so easily this time. You've broken my heart with your betrayal."

Cain took in a ragged breath, barely withholding tears.

"Clearly, this simple appointment is too much for you. You've become distracted by the demands of these insects. Worry for them no longer, I will take care of all that. You, my love, must again earn my favor. I have given you love, I have given you ecstasy beyond the dreams of even the most hedonistic of kings. And still, your eye strays…"

Something writhed inside him, possessed him to cry out: "I have given you everything!"

"Not everything!" Thunder crashed; a pall fell over the room. In a discordant meld of masculine and feminine voices, Morgana whispered, "Your heart remains yours."

"No…"

"Descend the Stair. Unearth it. Present it to me."

"Please—"

"Bring me your beating heart!" Light returned to the room, her voice gentle again. "Only then will you be restored in my eyes. Only then will I invite you to stand by my side once more."

"At your side…."

"Where you belong."

The Dread Angel swept out of the room to carry on her wanton slaughter of the Monrovians, an extension of Cain's cruel punishment for his adultery, his daring to desire the woman who once held him and understood him like no other, and once wore a ring emblazoned with his house's sigil that now lay in a pile of viscera.

Syr Arthur Cain stumbled into the dark of night, mentally calling for his mount, and together they took to the skies on a fell errand—Morgana's Chosen set out fully intending to unbury his heart from where it rested in the deepest depths of Pandemonium. His matron—his mistress—owned his soul, and thus his freedom to choose, but as they flew farther from her storms, from her hold, the fog strangling his better judgment began to fade.

Soaring over the Congealed Sea, he heard a derelict vessel splinter to pieces and the piercing scream of a woman calling his name. He looked down, locked eyes with his daughter, dangling from the shaft of a harpoon, impaled in a great serpent, mere seconds from her second death.

But Morgana's fog clung to his mind, as it had long lingered there like a foul odor setting into a blanket. He shook his head, trying to dislodge the fingers prying at him—always prying and pulling and demanding foul things of him he did not wish to give!

Cain saw the light leave his daughter's green eyes as he soared past her, watched Kateryna give up and let go of her meager hold on whatever hope had dared to remain. He had seen that same deflation, that same defeat in Anastasia, when he told her the king had ordered him to march against the Kaza'dur.

The haze burned away.

"Not again!" Cain yelled, a battle cry—a promise. "Never again!"

Gritting his teeth, Cain pulled on the reins and commanded Montauk to dive. He leaned forward and low to cut through the misty air. Cain held open his arms, and Kateryna smashed into him, sending Montauk spinning, nearly crashing into the bitter waves.

Once stabilized and safe from the hunger of the serpent, Kateryna opened her eyes. Recognition, then confusion, spread over her face. Clearly, she had expected to wake up to a whole new hell.

"You… you came back," she croaked before she was overtaken by a fit of hollow coughs.

"Yes," Cain said, holding her tight, so that she did not fall from the saddle. "I did."

* * *

In the Vale Betwixt—once a place between worlds meant to ease the soul's transition into death, now an underworld desiring to hoard their boundless energy—Morgana's eyes are everywhere. They weep from storm clouds at nearly every minute of nearly every day. They overwhelm those who toil beneath their scrutiny—not that many still did, I can assure you of that, dear reader.

Surely, the Goddess Corrupted witnessed her lover's final betrayal, which must have burned her in an unknowable way, I hope never to dream of. Had she still been in Monrovia, she might have taken flight to end him, once and for all. But when her many eyes reported his treachery, she had already returned to the comfort of her seat—her rightful place atop the Scarlet Chair.

The ground pulsed like heartbeat, and the Goddess Corrupted decided to let him find his own end, for surely his path could end only in demise. Another pulse; she shivered, pressing her thighs together for an instant, then regained her composure before the ever-plotting heathens in her court noticed her flash of weakness.

Morgana lifted her chin, ever so slightly, so that she looked down on all who appeared before her. Her expression was unreadable. There were more important matters for her to attend to. She would send the *others* after him.

* * *

I woke, dear reader, to find my hovel flooded.

The town was devoid of life and slowly sinking. Disbelieving all that I had seen, I weaved the sorcery of transposition, and I opened a gate. I fled Pandemonium to lick my wounds and to ponder my aching thoughts.

Do not be fooled. I am a coward, most foul. A wizard who is not, is not a wizard for long. Always trust your instincts, always listen to your intuition. These things keep you alive, and your soul—safe!

III

A conversation, somewhere far away.

Are you remembering now? I hope so, for all our sakes.

Understand, my friend, everything is riding on you. Rest will come, but only after you've finished your errand. Now rise, stretch your legs. Time is short, and there's still much to cover.

Three weeks after your sixteenth name day, Ibrahim was waiting for you in your chambers. He told you the elders were sending you to Valencia, the city of gold. The Golden City was much smaller then, little more than a stout fortress tucked between the three great mountains damming the South Sea and the Black, far from the world power it has become.

You begged him to stay; he didn't want to send you.

"This is the only way I can ensure you survive," Ibrahim had said. "Our chapel is not long for this world."

"I can't!" you cried. "Dusk teaches love above all... And you would send me to fight?"

Ibrahim showed his teeth, but you knew it was not a grin in truth. Behind that mask, you saw grief consuming him. "Dusk loves her children, my son. This is why she commanded us to send you and the others away. Yes, you will fight. But you will have a chance that the rest of us will not."

"I'll stay. I choose to die." You said, eyes bright with conviction. "I will not leave you."

The old man backhanded you for that. Your smooth cheek burned where his hard knuckles struck.

"Do not defy me! You are my pupil—more important, you are my son! I claimed you as my own so you could live!" When he saw your tears, he softened. "You are still a boy. You have so much yet to learn… but I cannot teach you. Our time has run out. My poor boy, I am so sorry, manhood must be thrust upon you now, of all times. But you must answer the call with grace. You must trust that the Great Mother will guide you. You must survive to carry our flames into the night."

Ibrahim clasped you in a warm embrace. It was the first time you've felt such warmth from another. Your true father was not an affectionate man, nor was your mother a tender woman—such treats they reserved only for each other, and never extended these gifts to you.

You heaved, trembling in Ibrahim's arms, knowing only too well what it means to see someone for the last time.

You and five others were smuggled away from the chapel in the dead of night. The priests delivered you to a remote dock on a lagoon along a major ocean trade route. An Ionian captain with a thick oiled mustache had his deckhands stuff you all in fish barrels for safekeeping.

The Kaza'dur controlled the northern tip of Skan'basan—the governor of your unnamed colony was among the first to adopt the new regime.

"Don't you worry!" came the captain's muffled voice above the lid of your barrel. "I'll get you lot to the Golden City in one piece—and there you will win glory!"

After a long, sickening voyage, your party was delivered to the captain of the Valentine guard in exchange for a silken purse swollen with coin.

In the barracks, you learned most of the Imperial forces were scattered to the wind, lost navigating the sprawling dunes of the unnatural erg that came with the arrival of the Kaza'dur. That land had once hosted a green, lush deciduous forest.

Now it was arid, a true sand sea implanted in the northern hemisphere.

Casualties were so high that the Valentine Governor resorted to buying young orphans to helm the walls. The city guard was a mere two hundred strong, most of them seeing no more battle than a street brawl. This scant company, joined by a troupe of displaced youths, was all that lay between the Kaza'duran invaders and the heart of the Empire.

You had but a day to rest, then your training began.

Scouts reported a siege force approaching. They were to arrive in just two weeks. Yet in those two weeks, you discovered something within yourself, a natural affinity for combat that you never possessed with words. You shed your youthful padding; your face slimmed and hardened; your arms swelled from long days hefting spears with lead weights affixed to their heads.

The camaraderie you knew between your fellows who had sailed the South Sea had kept you breathing during unending days and sleepless nights. You traded quill and papyrus for spear and shield. You became a soldier. Dusk's gentle touch in that hot spring was a fading memory. You craved battle, driven to find honor in the glory of liberating your people.

For six months, the Kaza'dur laid siege over the Golden City. Though the white walls held against the tide, the losses were overwhelming. Two of your companions perished; a boy was run through on the parapet, and a girl withered from starvation.

I will not burden you with the details of the conflict. There was nothing honorable nor glorious in what occurred during those long months. There were memories even I couldn't uncover, and I can't blame you for wishing to keep them buried.

However, there is an image of a woman, a healer, you first saw amputating a man's leg after he was struck by a barbed arrow. She was a beacon, a light in the carnage, her fair skin reflecting the overwhelming sunlight. You marked her as a foreigner by her clear azure eyes, a signature trait among the striders of the Wyse.

Nothing is certain in the heat of battle, but you hoped to see her again—and you did, the next day, after you took a pike in your shoulder. You felt that warm spring water lapping on your skin as she brought you back from the Great Mother's grasp.

After a series of hard-fought battles and a lot of luck, Valencia's scant defenders pushed back the invaders, forcing their retreat back into the Endless Sands, as the desert had come to be called.

With so many lying dead, the four of you from Dusk's chapel across the sea were named and knighted in the Valentine tradition. In the towering, extravagant cathedral dedicated to the Dusk and Dawn, Lord Governor Esteban Vidoq laid the flat of his gilded longsword upon your backs. The knights who rose before him were dubbed Syr Gabriel, Syr Derrida, and Dame Citha.

You rose as Syr Arthur.

The cathedral seemed like it might crumble beneath the thunder of applause, but everything fell silent to your ears as you glimpsed those northern blues watching you from the crowd of faceless onlookers.

After the ceremony, she stood alone on the balcony overlooking the Bell Quarter. People danced in the streets below, singing in myriad languages the praises of their stalwart defenders, who stood tall against mortal odds. The cityscape was breathtaking, a view unlike any other, its people and their candles pulsing like vigorous blood in the veins of a giant of myth—but you didn't see any of that.

Your heart fell into the pit of your stomach as you imagined her turning to look at you with those eyes you'd thought might remain accessible only in your dreams.

You leaned on the railing next to her.

She pretended not to notice.

You stood in silence for an uncomfortable moment. You were used to being spoken to—or rather, spoken at—and so you had no notion what to say.

"Thank you," was all you could manage.

It was the first time you'd spoken to anyone in the Golden City without being addressed first. You were a knight now—you had become a man.

She looked up at you, her expression indecipherable. Your heart skipped a beat as she placed a slender, callused hand atop yours. The gesture was so forward, so improper to the delicate sensibilities of the Valentines—and it drove you wild.

"I'm Anastasia," she said, her voice a sweet harmony, heavily accented. "You should know the name of the woman who saved your life."

"Yes…"

You had no clue what to say next; you were lost in her gaze, which must have seen the world to have arrived there. You imagined a sprawling, frozen landscape, from the northern reaches to the southern edge and the eastern shores.

Who was this woman, you wondered? Was she nymph or muse? No, my friend, she was just a woman—and she was all you wanted from that point hence. You absorbed her features, her long, dark hair flowing to her lower back in thick braids, her subtle curves whispering through her plain clothes, dotted with blood.

Her raised brow pulled you from your reverie. This woman would have you speak—and speak well!

So you spoke: "Arthur."

Her lips curling upward relieved you of the itching anxiety that you may have misread her.

"That's what the Valentines named you. I want to know what your mother named you."

"I relinquished all other names when I devoted myself to Dusk."

Anastasia snorted. "Ridiculous! The name given to a babe is a sacred thing."

"Why is that?" You truly wanted to know. You yearned to understand everything about this woman and her foreign land and her foreign traditions. She was a yarn waiting to be unraveled, and you wanted to spend your life uncovering her secrets.

"On the Wyse," she sighed, taking a breath. Was it a painful memory that appeared behind her mask? "There is no telling if a child will live. When a child survives, they are given a name. It is earned. This marks them as worthy to live a full life."

"I've never thought about it that way."

"Of course not! You're from the south. Skan'basan, yes?"

"Yes. My colony fell years ago. My home…" You winced, remembering that warm embrace, now so far away. "Was taken in the invasion."

She exhaled, closed her eyes, and muttered incomprehensibly under her breath. Was it a prayer? Silence returned, and you both stood looking out at the revelry below, an air of mourning from your shared, unspoken losses.

"Cain," you said, not wanting a wall between you two ever again.

Anastaisa turned, her brilliant eyes sparkling in the moonlight.

You said it again. The word bites hard on your tongue. It was a sin to utter that name; you had relinquished it before the eyes of the Mother. But then you said it a third time. Suddenly, your greatest fear was disappointing this woman before you, and you'd commit every sin there was if it meant pleasing her.

Thankfully, she never asked that of you. Not her.

Never her.

"My name is Cain."

IV

In the fog of the Screaming Fields

The Vale Betwixt, first layer of Pandemonium

Kateryna shivered by the dwindling campfire. The air was temperate, at least compared to the gales on the sea, but her fever was worsening, and comfort had become an impossibility. Worse yet, her clothes were damp, reeking of waste now that she was on solid ground.

Solid ground.

For the first time since her first death, she was on solid ground. Earth, dirt, sulfur, the whole nine continents, and the seas between! *Do any of those things still exist?* She wondered if she still resided upon Earth—or was Pandemonium somewhere else altogether? So many questions swam through her mind at once, as if all her thoughts had piled up against Morgana's wall and spilled over in the moment it crumbled.

Cain sat across her, hunched over his sword as he ground a whetstone across its edge. Dense fog encroached on all sides. A mournful cry resounded in the mist, now and again. Someone in pain. Someone dying. Her eyes fell on Cain's blade.

It occurred to her then that she had no idea how Pandemonium worked. Scripture painted the Great Beyond and the Underworld as spiritual places, beyond the body. But there Cain was sharpening a sword. She, and everyone, and everything else, was as much flesh and bone as she had ever been. Hunger, thirst, disease, fatigue—it was the same.

No… it was worse.

Kateryna had languished in Monrovia so long that suffering became the norm, beneath her notice; every emotion and sensation, every thought and worry—everything had remained below the surface and never survived long enough to blossom.

The suffering and the toil were the least of it. Above all, Pandemonium isolated its victims, separating them from everything that made them whole.

Kateryna closed her eyes and rubbed her hands in the cool dirt. When she was a girl, the country around the estate was completely wild save for narrow dirt paths and a few wheat farms. She remembered coveting those early mornings when she snuck out from the walls to roll in the red grass and play in the dirt.

She had felt so connected to the world then, she had thought that she felt the Great Mother breathe—giving birth, taking life, starting the cycle anew. There, in Morgana's demesne, she felt nothing but a subtle, beating pulse. The land was dead, picked clean.

True hell is the place farthest from the gods.

An old scripture. She did not remember which.

Somewhere, a man screamed. There was no way to know how far or how close, but his rasp and subsequently smothered breath sounded all too near for Kateryna's liking. She imagined Seth somewhere out in the mist—hunted for sport.

The thought made her want to vomit, but she had already lost the entirety of her innards during the flight.

"Where are we?"

Cain looked up briefly from his work, then back down. "We call these parts the Screaming Fields." He slipped, slicing his finger on the blade. Wiping the blood on his trousers, he rose to sheathe his very sharp sword and to stow the whetstone in a loose saddle bag. "This is where the lost wander until they are devoured."

"Yes, that much is clear." Another scream rang out as if to punctuate the statement, a woman this time.

Kateryna shivered, everything about this place unsettled her to the core—as it was designed to do. "But what about the rest of it? Why are we dead but beholden to the needs of the living? How does any of this work?"

Cain looked up, as if searching for the answers behind the clouds. "I don't know."

"Since we died, it's been... years? Decades? All this time licking Morgana's boot, and you don't know how this place works?"

Cain shuddered at the utterance of the Dread Angel's name. His eyes traced a path between the fog and the blackened dirt at his feet. Recognition lit up in his eyes, followed by a spread of realization. "Before now... I've never thought about it. I was not allowed to."

Kateryna fought the urge to scream at him then, if only to avoid luring some terrible demon to devour them. Her throat was a shredded mass of ribbons, so she was unlikely to muster the voice, anyhow. Rage bellowed deep within, calling for reprieve. She was about to say something nasty—it was the least she could do to strike back—but the look in his black eyes gave her pause. His expression was not one of thoughtless ignorance, but of sudden epiphany. Kateryna watched the glaze seep from the whites of his eyes as his gaze settled on her.

He is seeing. Perhaps for the first time, he sees me.

"Yes," Cain continued, squatting next to her. "We've been living in hell... We're dead, and have been for a long time."

Kateryna had no clue what to say to that. Instead, she was consumed by a rib-clenching coughing fit as she opened her mouth. She clutched her chest, doubled over, hacking and wheezing. When finally she regained her composure, there was a puddle of black blood, pooled in the shape of a star beneath her.

"You should have let me drown…" she groaned. "At least that way I could have continued on without this damned plague."

Cain shook his head. "That would have been no better. This place is vast; you'd have been lost, and I'd have to find you too. That, and there's no telling what terrible form awaited you."

Kateryna pushed herself back onto her haunches. "You're…" She almost had no will to say it, to invite the same disappointment with which she had become so intimate in this unnatural life. "You're going to help me find her?"

Without hesitation, Cain said: "Yes."

A gust of wind roared in the sky, joined by an avian caw growing louder. Cain's raven-like monster landed with a thud next to him. It dropped a grotesque, rotting eel at his feet.

Cain smiled, scratched the creature under the chin until it flopped over on its side like a bison-sized house cat. The sight was nothing short of ridiculous; a man, who had until then been a constant antagonist in her life, giving a monster affectionate scratches.

"Kateryna," he said, waving her over. "This is Montauk. It's important you two meet properly."

She reluctantly inched towards them. The monster—Montauk—rolled onto its feet and backed away as she drew near.

"Careful, she's slow to trust."

Something I can relate to.

"It's a she?"

He grinned at her then, to which Kateryna did not know how to respond. "Of course. Also, she doesn't like being called *it.*"

"What should I do?"

"Hold out your hand."

An image of her hand severed at the wrist came to mind; Cain, lifeless, staring ambivalent, disinterested daggers into her corpse as she bled in the dirt. It seemed to her a reasonable anxiety, given every prior interaction she had had with the bastard.

Giving up every call to reason, Kateryna held out her hand.

Montauk only stared at first, narrow slit eyes moving between Kateryna's face and tremulous fingers, but then the griffin drew closer and sniffed her hand. She heard a low rumble as Montauk moved to nudge her shoulder—*Gods in hell and up above, she's purring!*

Cain watched silently from a careful distance.

Kateryna looked at him; he nodded his approval. Montauk dipped her massive head between Kateryna's legs, tossing her into the saddle. Despite herself, Kateryna giggled. It reminded her of childhood—those mornings alone, rolling down hills. Decades ago, maybe more. Another life.

"She likes you," Cain said.

"Yes!" was all Kateryna could manage as the griffin bucked like a rambunctious hound. She grabbed the saddle horn and felt something smooth. Looking down, there was a drop of fresh blood on it. "I want to get down now… alright, Montauk?"

The beast paid her no heed. Cain raised a fist, and the griffin halted instantaneously. Kateryna climbed down, fell back onto the ground, head spinning.

"She's a bit overzealous, sometimes," Cain said, scratching his head.

"It's not that…" she whispered, suddenly overwhelmed by a blizzard of emotions and pains and searing contradictions. Her heart thudded against her chest, her brain swelling inside her skull. "For so long, I've cursed you. Prayed for your second death."

She looked up at him, surprised to see his black eyes dejected.

"You abandoned us... even though you swore to my mother you would never leave us behind. You swore an oath before the light of the High Noon. Marriage is supposed to be binding, no?"

"Yes. It is."

An image of a newly carved tombstone came to her then, uninvited. An arch of lavender, unattended. She shook away those painful memories. *Not yet.*

"How do you expect me to trust you? At every turn, you've ignored me—or betrayed me!"

Cain's head sagged. "That's exactly what I've done."

Kateryna heaved, seized by another coughing fit. She crumbled to the ground, feeling like she might soon become one with the sulfuric soil. Her blooming migraine spiked, and suddenly she was rattled by chills.

"Kat!"

The world spun round and round, and blackness swallowed her all at once.

Minutes passed—or hours, who could tell?—before Kateryna awoke, Montauk curled around her like a mother lion with her cub. She was wrapped in a knit blanket she had not seen since before her first death. The yarn was stiff and ratty, but the color was still vibrant. *Mother knitted this when I was still toddling.*

Cain stood vigil beyond the threshold of the camp. His back was to her, his sword drawn.

The incessant screaming in the distance had ceased for the moment, and so too the miasmic nausea that had plagued her since leaving Monrovia. Kateryna settled back into the warmth of the purring griffin. *Will you earn my trust, father?* She was unsure. So much had changed.

But evil and pain were all that hell could promise....

V

From the collected journals of a mad wizard

When first I returned home, I thought I might be free of those hellish nightmares. Wishful thinking, really; the stench of Pandemonium lingers, and no amount of soap nor baths did anything to remove it from my tainted, mortal flesh.

My heart dripped with worry. I feared for poor Kateryna, and I was captivated by Cain's betrayal of his beloved matron.

I had arrived in my quarters by way of advanced transposition—not instantaneous, more like a tunnel leading directly to your destination. Such travel is exhausting and time-consuming, especially when folding between layers of reality. I spent the next several hours meticulously weaving wards into every inch of every wall, into every blanket, chair, door, window, anything that held any chance of carrying a curse or plague-ridden bacteria.

When finally I lay my weary head upon my pillow, I crumpled into my mattress like a bag of bones. But there was no rest awaiting me in slumber. No, dear reader, I did not need even to cast an incantation for prophetic dreams of hell to find me. They came on their own, unwelcome and insistent.

I found myself back in Pandemonium, standing in what I intuited as the hall of Morgana's keep. When I cast my oneiromancy, I can maintain complete control of my perspective, and oft I opt for a bird's-eye view to avoid detection

by my subjects. But since I saw through the eyes of the
Goddess Corrupted, I no longer had control of the dreams. I
was standing in someone else's shoes, in a memory, or perhaps
experiencing that moment simultaneously.

* * *

Kneeling, I felt the heat radiating from the floor through
my poleyns. In Morgana's court, the walls were naked, built of
shimmering, black granite. There were paintings when we first
arrived, but she ordered them taken down... I will never know
why. Who can understand the machinations of the divine?

She had me kneeling like a dog for a long time, as though
testing me. Morgana glared, as if Arthur's stupidity was
somehow reflected in me. I was fucking terrified; I thought she
might have my head for the fun of it. I could not even fathom
what horror awaited me after a second death.

I had borne witness to much crueler fates than what the
poor sods in Monrovia knew. The gods only know what hell
they suffer now.

"I want him *gutted*. I want him *burned*. I want every trace
of his thrice-damned existence reduced to *ash*!" Morgana raged,
her cacophonous voice storming through the hall, shaking the
walls. Then, all sound ceased, the quivering walls stilled, and a
terrible chill deeper than the Wystran winter limed the hall with
black-frosted hate. "Do you understand me, Syr Derrida?"

"Yes, mistress," I said. My voice was a rasp; I felt like my
vocal cords had hemorrhaged. "I will inform the others."

"Go."

Morgana sat upon her throne. Lord Sanguine had
apparently dubbed it the Scarlet Chair, which never made
sense to me—the damned thing was made of tarnished copper,
patinated sea-foam green. Veins undulated between the jagged
peaks making up the throne's back. I always wondered if it was
somehow alive.

The corner of Morgana's lip quivered. A flash of discomfort,
corrected in an instant.

I had noticed such… slips, occurring with growing frequency, and I found myself mourning my matron's state. She had once been so pure, beyond the limits of the human condition. Now, like an aging housewife, she was sending us to wreak petty vengeance on a mortal man.

"You are now my Herald, Derrida," Morgana purred, tilting her chin up ever so slightly, and tilting the rest towards me, ever so slightly. "Do this, and I will reward you graciously…"

Hunger stirred within. I never dared fantasize about having Arthur's place by her side—that would be blasphemy. But now, the Goddess had called me only by that name which she bestowed upon me, and stoked my desire with her divine will. *Or I had done that myself. How does one resist?*

"Thank you, mistress."

She bade me to rise, and so I did, and rushed out from Morgana's hall, ascending darkened stairwells and traversing sharp corridors with inhuman urgency. My mind swam with the possibilities before me. The world was mine for the taking.

As I drew further into the keep, my loins calmed, and I was left with an unwelcome, intrusive thought. *I don't think I can kill Arthur.* I was not nearly so skilled in combat as he—or anyone, for that matter—but moreover, he was my friend. *But she is my Goddess, and she offers me her hand, which that fool squandered.*

I was dumbfounded by his stupidity.

The Goddess loved him, clearly. She would not send us after him if it were not so. He had scorned her, and somehow, he had wounded her. *Arthur chose a mortal woman over the Goddess.* That part I could not wrap my head around. In life, my wife was a pleasant woman, and she birthed me two sons, but we married for political gain. Our indifference was mutual, and I had not spared her a thought since awakening in Morgana's service.

And now Morgana might give her love to me. The stirring returned, and I imagined what wonders lingered beneath those perfect dark silks and blackened armor plates. Such a sight would be too much for mortal eyes—I might go blind. *A risk I'm willing to take.*

In the aerie at the top of the keep, my comrades—now underlings—tended to their mounts. Citha, a lithe Skanu clad in sleek brigandine, fed living trout to her griffin, which took the aspect of a gyrfalcon. I have always been attracted to her exotic features; her thin, corded musculature, her tight braids, smooth umber skin. Alas, the legendary Dame never looked twice at me. *Not that I need her affectations—not after Arthur's through.*

Gabriel, a great, bloody ox of a man, groomed his incongruous condor griffin. I had little hope of winning his loyalty, despite our matron naming me Herald. I hoped he would not pose a problem.

My own mount, beautifully crafted by our matron in the aspect of a Kaldean eagle, nudged my shoulder. He sensed my unease. I sighed deeply, shook out my hands in preparation for the reaming I was about to receive from these two.

"Our matron demands blood," I said, shifting in my stretched and torn boots, now too loose on my feet. "We take to the skies immediately."

Dame Citha scoffed. "We don't take orders from you."

I swallowed. *I need to keep my cool.* "I have been named Herald. Now, mount up! We must ride."

"Who died and made you so gods-fucking important?" said Syr Gabriel, towering over me. He bent down and prodded my chest with a finger the size of a sausage. How I loathed Gabriel, the shit-crusted whoreson.

"Arthur is marked for death. We must depart now if we are to catch up with him before he crosses the Goddess's threshold."

Citha and Gabriel exchanged worried glances.

"It was only a matter of time before she found out what he was up to." Citha said.

Gabriel took a step back, gracing me with an inch or two to breathe. "He went home to his wife, eh? Bloody fool."

I nodded. "You know how our mistress prefers this done—silver through the heart, silver through the brain."

"Too bad," Gabriel went on. "He was a good Herald. Better than you'll be, I reckon."

You're not wrong, there, buddy ol' pal.

Citha patted her griffin on the head, then swept onto her saddle in a single fluid motion. She closed her eyes, muttering some old Skanu prayer that had long since lost its power in the Vale Betwixt.

My mount shifted his weight between his front legs, whining softly until I placed a hand on his forehead. "Hush now, Krakow…" My boy was an empath, always anxious when I was. "Everything will be fine."

Gabriel and I retrieved our saddles and weapons from the wall and geared up. We sat in silence for a time before taking off. There was a shift in power, and all of us felt it—none of us knew who would survive to benefit from it. I nodded at Gabriel, and he and his grotesque monster bounded through the landing bay into the open sky. I followed, Citha taking up overwatch at the rear. I hoped Gabriel felt my glowering hot on his back.

I will be the one, this time. Me.

THREE

You have been robbed.
Of something.
You didn't know.
Could be taken.

Syr Arthur Cain (-13 to 35)
"Awakening," published Year 36.

I

A conversation, somewhere far away.

The Kaza'dur left a gross power vacuum in their wake. In the years following your knighthood, you rose through the ranks of Valentine Aristocracy.

Valencia was no longer a humble fortress, subservient to a crumbling empire. The Kaldean capital, the Great City of Baltaire, fell the instant the invasion began. Once the Lord Governor Vidoq perished of dysentery, Don Laszlo Balderas the First put a crown upon his head and declared himself High King of "New Kaldea"—the name never stuck, as you know—elevating the Golden City to a superpower, as it was the sole producer of grain and wine to the surviving Kaldean cities.

High King Balderas financed the construction of three new fortresses along the southern borders of the Valentine Outlands. He had hoped these might prevent those wretched snakes from ever again approaching the white walls of Valencia.

On the first morning of spring, marked by dense cadres of daffodils bursting from every inch of soil and dancing robins courting in the open air, a ceremony was held in your honor.

Well, yours and two of your companions. Together, you and Syr Gabriel and Syr Derrida stood before the High King, who named each of you Lord Protector and bestowed upon you a border-keep. You swore an oath before the Dusk and Dawn, by light of the High Noon, to give your life if necessary in the fight against the invaders.

Dame Citha watched on from the front row, a grimace painted across her face, aimed unwaveringly at Derrida's chest. When he felt her indignation, he deflated beneath the weight of his newly bequeathed golden badge. Derrida knew he was selected by merit of his cock—not for his ability to command.

Citha knew this, and so did you.

The slender man swallowed ash, on display for every Valentine Noble to scrutinize. He dreaded the dire responsibility that would come with his castle. Worse, he crumbled beneath the resentment of a woman he held overwhelming, unrequited love for.

Your keep was the closest to the city, so naturally, you all enjoyed a sumptuous dinner in your lavish dining hall. Centering the room was a great longtable made from four ancient sycamores. Lining the walls were stout pillars of polished limestone.

The High King had commissioned Astrofus, a renowned philosopher and sculptor—also a hack, but that's beside the point—to festoon the entire room with hand-carved renders of Kaldean heroes in perfect marble. The affair had cost millions and stirred up quite the controversy among the nobility.

"Just think," Gabriel cried out, raising an ivory tankard of spiced blueberry mead, "not long ago, we were filthy waifs shoved into fish barrels to serve as live bait on the walls!"

"Gods... how things can change," said Derrida, running his hand across a marble woman's bodice.

"Gods?" You shook your head in disbelief. "You borrow too much from these Valentines."

Citha nodded her agreement, muttering a quick prayer to Dusk under her breath.

Gabriel leaned forward, spilling mead on the new table. "Don't tell me you still believe all that shite the monks went on about? Come now, Arthur! It's all a bunch of superstitious rubbish!"

"We've been blessed—some of us well beyond what he deserves," Citha said, glaring at Derrida, who ducked behind his marble woman. "And you dare to blaspheme by belittling our generous Goddess?"

"Blaspheme? Blaspheme!" Gabriel rose, throwing his tankard splashing to the floor. "What's fucking blasphemy are the fucking snakes who just decided on a whim that our world belonged to them! Where was your 'generous Goddess,' then?"

"We have been knighted by Dusk's holy decree! Given sacred names of renown and land to call our own!" Citha's eyes went wide. "In what godless world would four orphans be given so much?"

"Damn it, woman. Again with the bloody hysterics!" Gabriel stormed out of the hall without another word.

You hadn't known he felt that way. You had thought Dusk revealed herself to all her children. Now, you were beginning to doubt even that. Though the memory of that night in the hot spring was slowly eroding, you never questioned the certainty you felt at Dusk's gentle touch.

"I'm sorry, Citha. That was uncalled for."

She snorted, lips curled at the sound of Gabriel's heavy footsteps echoing deeper in the keep. "You are not who need apologize."

"I allowed him to disrespect you and our faith in my home. I should have intervened."

"Arthur," Citha sighed, her dark eyes trained on yours, "there are other women in your life to worry over. I don't need you to defend me."

You looked to Derrida for support. Poking out from his hiding place, he only shrugged. You smiled, glad most of your companions remained your friends.

* * *

Anastasia sat in a patch of lilies and daffodils outside the walls. The hills, usually golden brown with dashes of red, were covered in waves of rolling green grass. She held her belly, swollen with child. You placed a gentle hand on her shoulder and watched proudly as your daughter played in the grass, hunting for beetles.

Despite the tranquility of the moment, your heart was steeped in worry.

The first pregnancy had been challenging for Anastasia; she nearly didn't make it through. She was underweight then, and she was thinner now. She had become the Lady of a castle—she should have been comfortably plump and full-bodied. Irrational though it was, you blamed yourself for failing to provide, as if lack of food were the sole culprit behind her failing health.

She sensed your unease, danced her hand atop yours. Her touch had a way of quelling your anxieties. You bent down, pressed your chapped lips against hers. They were soft, tasting faintly of honey. Her mouth vibrated as she hummed a sigh of relief, as if your presence were as soothing as a cool cup of water on a summer's midday.

"Only yesterday it seems she learned how to walk," you said, admiring your little girl again. You could never keep your eyes off her for long. "Now she's running through the grass, cherishing every life she comes across."

"Isn't she gorgeous, Cain?" Anastasia said, her voice the plucking of a harp to your ears. "This world isn't ready for the gifts she'll give."

Kateryna bent down, offered her stubby finger to the Monarch butterfly. She screeched with delight when it instead landed atop her long, ginger curls.

"No…" You said, a smile set deep in your hard face. "The world isn't ready."

* * *

That day would live on in your dreams.

You didn't know what Dusk's afterlife might look like, but you hoped it meant reliving that afternoon on the hill, time and time again.

I'm so sorry that wasn't what happened.

You were a soldier, you knew the risks you took, but you never thought your devotion would destroy your girls—your unborn child. The Dread Angel's malice knew no bounds; she laid claim to your eternal soul and stole those of your family.

The days following that peaceful afternoon in the rolling, wheat-laden hills marked the rising swells that would grow into waves battering the tranquil shores of your life. You suffered the consequences of events that had occurred well before your time and, by right, had nothing to do with you. Is it your fault, Morgana's Chosen, that the Goddess Corrupted marked you as her unyielding favorite amidst a sea of countless devotees? Did you invite her eye, tempt her to abandon the ways of godhood for the excess of mass consumption?

Do you remember the nightmare you had before you were called again to march upon the Kaza'dur? No?

It was a warm, late summer night, not four months since you'd moved into your holding. Sleep had found you easily, despite your anxieties of leaving Anastasia to give birth on her own, and her chronic condition that only seemed to worsen with each passing moon. You closed your eyes to find yourself back in the hot spring, floating in the warm water.

At first, a memory—a reminder of the first time you felt the love of another. You were only a boy, then, and you had possessed no notion of what you had truly promised to the goddess all those years ago.

Then, you felt her warmth. Dusk was in the water with you. Something deep in the recesses of your soul stirred. The goddess bade you to repeat the oath you had recited when first you met.

"I will never stop loving…" Suddenly, you felt a tinge of dishonesty in the words that followed.

Finish the verse, my Chosen.

"I will devote myself—"

No. You couldn't say it. You were devoted to another, now. You'd made a pact by light of the High Noon, and the world had been in attendance.

Say it, Arthur. You swore to me.

"I cannot..."

Your breath catches in your throat as your entire being is assaulted with overwhelming, otherworldly warmth and turgid desire. You beg for it to stop—painful delectation, agonizing ecstasy, a perverse multitude of sensations that numb your extremities.

Your folly is laid out before you, an argument of stimulation insisting that any promises you made after the goddess claimed your soul are null. You believe that for a moment, as the pleasure ascends to its fell climax, your stomach cramps and your legs shudder.

The temperature of the water rises; you're feverish and powerless and captivated all at once. You do everything to resist, to reject the sensations beset upon you, to find no pleasure in what is happening to you. Your skin is clammy and raw, your muscles are aching, and you scream your protest.

All to no avail.

No one is listening. The goddess assaults you, uninhibited.

It's too much, you are only human, you are only a mortal man—and men are not to be trusted. You give in to the shame, to the voices shouting at you from all directions, demanding you give yourself over. Over to *her.*

She commands you to repeat your oath. You obey.

Your reward is a world-shattering release unlike anything you could have imagined—yet it is fleeting, soon replaced by heavy guilt congealing in your innards, settling at the bottom of your heart where it will remain for the rest of your days.

Your muscles relax; all sensation flees from your body, and you have been robbed of something you did not know could be taken.

When you woke, the moon still hung low in the night sky. Your wife sat weeping on the edge of the bed, facing away from you. Confused, bleary-eyed from sleep, you moved to embrace her—but stopped when you felt the mess under the covers.

Instead, you laid an uncertain hand on her shoulder. She shook it away, turned on you with the eyes of a stranger—eyes that had once enraptured your very soul, which now seemed to condemn it.

She opened her mouth, choked down a sob. Then, in a calm, even tone she asked: "Who is Morgana?"

II

In the sky, escaping Morgana's demesne

The Vale Betwixt, first layer of Pandemonium

Atop Montauk's back, soaring over the gray and dying lands that made up the Screaming Fields, the silver valley did not seem so dismal. Rushing by, the ground looked like a canvas, covered with a dark base of oils, yet to be rendered further. Pandemonium had no expression, no harmony, as the land of the living above. Monrovia had been a hovel, everything beyond its limits a deathtrap. Aside from the nauseating swell of waves and failing support pillars, all was still and lifeless in Morgana's demesne.

Ancient myths, stories Kateryna had heard as a child off the mouths of travelling raconteurs, told of the Vale Betwixt and the cool color of its perpetual sunset, of the brittle sway of the leaves dancing in the languid breeze. Fulcrum had once told Kateryna that the sea they lived on was the flooded River Acheron, which Morgana had laid waste to, separating the borderlands between Life and Death.

So much waste. Soil, once carefully cultivated, now overwatered to drown out any and all life. Why—for what?

Kateryna felt Cain's slow breath on the back of her neck. She was on edge with him so close, not yet accustomed to the notion that he was no longer her enemy—that he suddenly cared about his role as her father.

How is it we were pulled down with you, father? Did you sell our souls for your gain? Or was this all an unfortunate accident?

She shivered, shifted uncomfortably in the saddle, eyes trained again on the meager bloodstain besmirching the saddle-horn. *How long had it been there? To whom did it belong? How many people had this man cut down between his two lives?*

She buried all that—pushed it way down. None of those questions yielded helpful answers, nor did they help Kateryna to feel right about her new direction. All that mattered was that she found her mother. One way or another.

"Someone left ahead of me," Kateryna said, if only to distract herself from her worries. "He had a day's lead on me. He might be down below."

Cain grunted. "I've not seen another boat. Nor has Montauk."

"We haven't searched for one."

"No—but we'd have seen it. If it still sailed."

If it still sailed... Kateryna had come to the same conclusion the moment she laid eyes on the leviathan. *Where have you gone, Seth? Can I find you, too?* Probably not. That hurt.

"He would have perished if he stayed behind..." Cain said through clenched teeth. "The Goddess took them all."

Kateryna winced. *Because of me... I taunted her, drew her ire.*

"Where are we going?" she asked.

"I don't know yet. Pandemonium is massive. Not even I have seen all its corners."

"We need a map."

"There are no maps. At least, not ones we can read. I know someone who might give us direction, should his mood allow it." Cain pointed to a dark spot in the distance, hovering high in front of a gargantuan wall of light on the horizon. "He lives on the border of Morgana and Grahtzildahn."

She glanced back at him. "The Burning City…"

Cain nodded.

Kateryna watched as the threshold drew closer. Soon, she could make out the mosaic pattern of sea foam and shattered glass, barring the fogs of The Screaming Fields from mixing with the black soot clouds pressing in from the other side. The two underworlds warred for territory against unwavering borders, pressing them into a bitter, eternal stalemate. The undulating hills beyond the threshold reminded Kateryna of home—not as they were throughout her childhood, but as they had lain barren the day she returned home to find her family had long since perished.

"Can this someone be trusted?"

Cain forced a curt laugh. "No one can be trusted, Kat. But he may help us yet. We fly to the Oracle of Dawn, the only man who can still commune with the gods above."

More hours passed by, mostly spent in tense silence, interrupted by an occasional question from Kateryna and Cain's unsavory, honest answer. She was beginning to doze when they came upon a ramshackle hut lodged within the middle of the border threshold.

On one side, the hut was rotten, the wood panels swollen from the humidity of Morgana's demesne, and sickly grass wept from between the decaying thatch covering the roof. On the other side, the thatch was blackened, cooked by the blazing heat of Grahtzildahn radiating throughout the Demon King's realm. Some force of sorcery suspended the structure high in the air—perhaps it was the threshold that held it aloft, perhaps something else entirely. The sight pained Kateryna. For so long, she had toiled to raise her sagging village away from the encroaching tides, yet here was the solution to all their problems, not three days' journey away.

Montauk landed gracefully on the small porch, hardly big enough to hold her. Floorboards bemoaned their protest as Cain dismounted.

"Worry not," he said. "This place cannot be damaged—not by the likes of us, at least."

Cain opened the door, not bothering to knock, then strode into the inky darkness beyond.

Kateryna followed, her eyes widening as she saw the massive chamber within, much larger than the meager exterior structure implied. She wiped tears from her eyes as a thick aroma of smoldering frankincense and lavender battered her senses. *This is high sorcery, the stuff of dreams… or nightmares.*

It took some time for her eyes to adjust to the dim light, sourced from one hanging iron lantern, dancing with viscous shadow, pushing ever inward to snuff out what little light remained. Bamboo wind chimes hung motionless about the chamber, which seemed to expand endlessly into the void surrounding them. The door evaporated with a suppurating *pop!* as it settled shut behind them of its own accord.

A black man—a native of Northern Skan'basan, by his dress and complexion—sat cross-legged beneath the lantern. A bloodied bandage covered his face, save for his mouth. Patches of his skin had been flayed, leaving plots of gnarled, twisted pink quilting across what little flesh was revealed. He wore a ring on each finger of his right hand—one of tarnished gold, two of silver, one of oxidized copper, and the last of rusted iron. His rings were all missing their stones, sockets barren.

"You've returned…" the old man said, mildly amused. His voice rang out, deep and clear, unlike anything Kateryna had expected. "I was beginning to think you were forever lost."

Cain removed his boots, then sat on the floor across him. Kateryna did the same.

"And here I am."

"Yes… But you are not whole."

Cain was expressionless. "I'm not."

The old man flashed his large, ivory teeth, then turned as if to address Kateryna—as if he could see her. "Kateryna Cain of

Undton, the would-be governess of Daizeton. It is a pleasure to finally meet you."

Kateryna swallowed ash.

She had forgotten about that, and now that aspect of her life, long since passed, poured into the basin of her memory as an overeager cupbearer overfills a lord's chalice. *Oh gods...* An image of a freshly carved tombstone consumed her vision. *"Here lies the lord's eldest son,"* the stone had read. *He should have never looked twice at me.*

"And you, as well—" Kateryna was overtaken by a series of hollow coughs. She cleared her throat and finished: "And you, Oracle."

The old man chortled, threw an exasperated hand at Cain. "This is how you've introduced me? I am insulted!" He spat into a golden cup at his side, which rang like a bell. "My name, dear Kateryna, is Ibrahim, Prophet of Dawn, the Great Mother Birth, known to your ancestors as Bridget and known to mine as Umi'al-jamise! You can call her whatever you like; she is not a picky goddess... unlike her sister, the Lady of the Chair." He shot a sidelong glance at Cain, who shrank beneath the old man's scrutiny like a child scolded.

Cain looked away and did not say anything to defend himself.

Kateryna was also at a loss for words, then beset by another fit of coughing, mucus streaming down her face. Her awareness rolled in and out, her vision wavered.

A firm hand grasped her shoulder. "Sit up, child," Ibrahim said, not unkindly, "swallow this, and be still."

The rim of a bottle touched her lips. Bitter, viscous fluid seeped down her tattered throat. A cool wind touched the inside of her chest, and when it touched her stomach, the nausea and coughing ceased.

"Gods..." Kateryna whispered, wiping her mouth on her sleeve. "What is that?"

"Lilac and gooseberries, with a touch of honey." Ibrahim pinched the air to demonstrate.

She stared at him.

The old man guffawed and slapped his knees, his deep voice reverberating through the floorboards. "I am joking, of course. I must maintain some secrets, don't you think?"

"Enough!" Cain roared, startling Kateryna. "There isn't time for games. Where is my wife?"

A pall fell over Ibrahim's face. "You have a lot of nerve to demand anything of me, boy. What do you offer in return, hmm?"

Cain opened his mouth but had no answer.

"Nothing! It is the only gift you're capable of giving!" The old man spat again into his golden cup.

"What of me?" Kateryna said. "Surely, I have something to offer."

Ibrahim smiled, but it was a mournful expression. "Yes, child... You do."

"Tell me, then. To save my mother, there is no price too high."

"As you can see," Ibrahim gestured about the vast oblivion surrounding them, "I do not have much to keep me occupied. I yearn for a story, a memory, something to ponder and archive until my next guest arrives. I know all of Cain's—he has nothing more to hide from me, but you, dear Kateryna..."

"I am new to you."

"Yes—you are new."

"Take care in what you give to him," Cain said. "You might unearth more than you meant to. What follows can be painful. Sometimes opening the flood gates is just so—a flood."

"Okay." Kateryna nodded, surprised by the clarity and earnestness in her father's black eyes. "I understand."

Ibrahim leaned forward, clapping both of his bony hands on her shoulders. "Take off my coverings, and gaze into my eyes."

Kateryna unraveled the soiled bandages from the old man's face. He unfolded his heavy eyelids, and she gasped at what she saw. Brightness shimmered and subsumed her. Planets and galaxies surged to and from existence; clusters of stars and asteroids swilled all around. She then understood that her body was simply a vessel, containing the near-infinite potential of her soul. Beyond the body, the world as she knew it was simply a tomb buried beneath the ruins of countless civilizations.

In that brief moment, Kateryna was free of it all. She was dust, drifting beyond the moon, then she plummeted into a sea of memory to relive a hundred moments of a life long passed.

When next she opened her eyes, she wept. Ibrahim held her, comforting her as a father should. Cain watched mournfully beside her, silent. She felt his rough hand encompass hers in belated solidarity.

III

From the collected journals of a mad wizard

I spent days pacing the tiles of my quarters in the western wing of the Citadel. I spent days pondering the implications of my visions, searching desperately for the thread that tied together everything I had seen thus far. I knew that somehow, I was bound to the poor people in the Vale Betwixt, and that it was my responsibility to intervene.

My colleagues were thrilled that I had returned from my morose expedition, and they pounded on my doors throughout the day. Yet I ignored them. In truth, my soul was still in Morgana's possession, though my body had escaped. Each night, I lay awake dreading the baleful nightmare that might next plague my dreams. I dared not allow my colleagues to see me in such a degenerate state for fear that they would cast me out.

It had been weeks since last I bathed, for the bath house was several blocks away and surely, I would be spotted should I venture out. I stank of rotten eggs—the stench of sulfur. Bath or no, dear reader, the malodor of hell falls from the unclaimed. Yet, despite my own efforts with soap and cloth, I could not wash away my folly.

My soul was mine no longer, and thus, I was entrenched in a battle between Life and Death.

You, my dear reader, possess the fortune of hindsight. The fact you are reading my words, published and printed, is evidence enough that my fate was salvaged. So too, I was bound to my course—compelled to see it through.

It was the better part of a month before I worked up the nerve to weave my oneiromancy, to summon a dream of my own accord. I lit a bundle of frankincense and lavender in my urn to cleanse the air of malicious particles. I circled my bed with salt, skimmed from the surface of the Black Sea, a mile below my feet, for all eleven days of the academic week. Chanting the ancient words of the arcane, I called for the answers I sought.

The moment I closed my eyes, I was dragged into another world—another time.

* * *

Standing on the peak of a gentle hill, I looked out unto a vast sea of rolling, rubrous, golden grasses. The land dipped and bucked, falling and rising with thick, spiky heads of wheat bulging with ample grain. This sight had once made me profoundly happy. Today, however, I was consumed with apprehension.

I unfurled my slender fingers, my nails trimmed but lined with dark soil. In my callused palm lay a gleaming ring of white gold, set with a swollen garnet. I wiped my eyes; no direction felt like the right one, and I was stuck idling away in my ambivalence.

Sucking a breath of dry, late summer air, I felt a hint of peace—if only in the familiarity of the heat, the wind battering me as if I had opened the wrought-iron door to a furnace, a blanket of sweat and fatigue the only comfort of the season.

I took one last glimpse at the land, sprawling and free, then turned around. In the distance, perhaps a league or so, a rugged keep sat awaiting my return. Much farther beyond the keep stood the looming spires of Valencia, as they stood just before the fall of the Empire and immediately after, before the first Laszlo had built them higher, after the invaders were defeated.

I had come out here and pondered my escape every day for the last month and had yet to enact my plot. I did not know if ever I might work up the courage. I sighed and began the long trek home.

My mother was sitting at the head of the dining table when I arrived, staring aimlessly at the wall. She had become so frail, fallen so ill since father left us to fight the invaders. Her once-sumptuous brunette curls had dried into wispy cords. Her blue eyes that had seen so much had fallen into the sockets and glossed over. A dull, familiar ache in my gut beset me as I rubbed my mother's shoulders and whispered gently into her ear.

"The monarchs are migrating, mother," I said as if coaxing a child to spend time outdoors. "We should walk to the meadow and watch, like we used to."

But my mother only sat there, her eyes now affixed on the old portrait hanging above the hearth. She and my father looked so healthy, so content, holding me as a newborn.

"I'll have someone brew a pot of chamomile," I said, forcing out the words, feigning compassion as I had for years now.

Air whistled through my mother's teeth as her exhalation escaped her. "Why, Kat? Why did he leave us? What have I done wrong?"

"You did nothing wrong!"

She wept at the escalation of my volume, her cries a stuttering staccato that she no longer attempted to withhold. I shook my head, the muscles in my jaw tensing as I pulled my mouth flat, so she did not see my vexation.

I was so tired, so exhausted. And I had had enough.

I marched to the hearth, then pulled down the damnable portrait, pulling the mounting peg out of the plastered wall, leaving behind a gaping wound above a second peg, which briefly held a different portrait before the one I grasped was solemnly replaced.

"What—what are you doing?" My mother cried, rising from her seat for the first time that day.

I only snarled and threw the painting into the hearth, glaring into my father's uncaring black eyes as his bitter countenance was consumed by hellfire. The flames crackled, the paint sizzled; together, they hissed: *"You'll burn, too."* I silenced the jeering with a fire poker, thrusting the iron tip through my father's expressionless mask until my mother pulled helplessly at my sleeves.

"Why?" she wailed. "Am I not tortured enough? My only child…" She fell to her knees before the smoldering canvas and did not move again until her chambermaids retrieved her after midnight.

The next morning, I stood before the full-body mirror in my mother's dressing room. I hardly recognized myself. I should have felt utterly vacillated, thrilled to walk the aisle into my own home, my own life. Away from my withering mother, who had begun to drain me alongside herself.

I should have been blessed with beautiful certainty. Instead, I scrutinized every detail of my pearly white gown.

Truly, the garment was gorgeous, immaculate, and befitting of the measured poise a governess should exude. But when I looked at the woman wearing it, saw her braided auburn locks, all I saw were the frizzled infant hairs jutting obstinately out of place. I stared into her freckled face, still scarred from youthful pocks and the fishing hook that had caught her cheek as a girl. I watched her pale, gray eyes—nothing like the resplendence my mother's own once held—travel the length of my awkward, muscular body.

Any other woman could fill this dress and would better live up to the precedent it set. Any other woman would better serve my betrothed and his people.

The man I was to marry was kind, stately; *gallant,* as the wards, daughters of minor houses, liked to say. And who was I? The daughter of an orphan and a nomad, the girl who played

with bugs and the woman who chops her own wood for the
fire, who fishes for her own food and prepares her own dinners.
Yes, I was bestowed a title at birth—but I was no lady. I had
no manners, nor did I have the poise and the tact of a proper,
noble lady.

"He deserves a better woman…" I said to the empty room,
as my mother could not be bothered to leave her bed on my
wedding day. "He deserves someone beautiful and decisive and
regal… Not me…"

I wanted to be the one, to be his wife, to fill that dress with
wide, child-bearing hips and ample breasts that could feed my
sons and daughters. Yet the seams were too tight around my
shoulders and stomach, and too loose around my chest. The
corset suffocated me, siphoned my breath, even though life had
already stolen every bit of air from my sails—and I had nothing
more to give.

I stared at that woman and made a decision.

I would not stand idle and let the tide of duty lay claim
to me; I would not make the same mistakes my father had. I
would stand up for my ideals—even if they were inherently
wrong. If I did not, no one else would.

Removing the white-gold ring from the third finger on my
right hand, I placed it gingerly on the nearby vanity. I stripped
off the flowing white gown I had no business wearing. I wiped
the paint from my face. I stripped myself of my right to vanity.
In its place, I donned my father's old tunic and leather riding
greaves, tied on a padded jerkin, and slid my hardened feet into
my worn leather boots that I had worn to travel every path and
hill within my father's holdings.

I slipped out the backdoor before the guests arrived for the
ceremony.

* * *

As I stirred from my summoned slumber, I was awakened
by someone pounding upon my front door. I rubbed the grit
and dried tears from my eyes, shaking my head. "Oh, my poor,

sweet Kateryna..." I mourned under my breath as I hurried to greet my impatient visitors.

Approaching the door, I was surprised to sense the presence of the Headmaster of the Citadel, Pascal Doon the Lavender. Dragons who walk in the shoes of men reek of sorcery and radiate heat, which feels much like sunlight—even through doors.

I had already begun reciting my salutations before I finished opening the door. "My dear friend! What draws you away from your busy schedule?"

"You've not left your quarters in the weeks since your return." Pascal Doon said as he stepped heavily over my threshold. His tone was eloquent and well-measured, yet his voice was guttural and primal, emanating from deep within his diaphragm. "The faculty is worried your expeditions have been too taxing on you. They desire to know if we need to solicit outside help to assist you in escaping your nightmares."

"Nightmares? I have no nightmares! I am on the cusp of a great discovery, a most venerable breakthrough! Nightmares? Bah! I laugh at the notion, Headmaster. Neigh—I scoff at it!"

"Could you share what you've found? I must know why you've been sequestered so."

I grumbled, crossing my arms. A cold draft licked my manhood, and I realized my loincloth had fallen off while I slept. Startled, I ambled to my wardrobe and hurried into a silken bathrobe.

"I will submit my research for peer review when it has been concluded. Be patient, you cold-blooded cur!"

A low growl rumbled in the back of my old friend's throat. "Understand, my friend, what follows is out of my hands. You've made your bed."

"What? I haven't made my bed in weeks!"

Two orderlies appeared on either side of me, taking hold of my arms. I was astounded that I had not smelled their sorcery.

Perhaps, I thought to myself, I was a bit worse for wear. My dawning understanding did not prevent my fruitless kicking and shouting of obscenities and draconic slurs.

It was far from my finest moment, dear reader.

"I need to know you're okay," Pascal Doon said calmly, after I had screamed my throat to ribbons. "We're taking you to the trial facilities. You will dream under our supervision. From there, we will present our findings to the faculty chair, and they will decide if you should continue this project."

The term "faculty chair" enraged me. Despite my bleeding throat, I began another litany. "You bastard! You can't censor me; I bloody built this place, brick by bloody brick! My mind is hammer and chisel, my word is law, my findings established sorcery as we know it! You fools are keeping me from witnessing the most significant metaphysical event in recorded history!" And on and on I went, frothing at the mouth as the orderlies dragged me through the western wing's halls, where the most esteemed professors lived and heard my mad tirade.

I have since grown to appreciate that my friend was only trying to help me. I even thanked him for his intervention and empathy. Eventually. Understand, dear reader, I had not slept for nearly a month—truly slept, for the sake of rest and recouperation—and I had developed an unhealthy obsession regarding my parasocial friends in Pandemonium and my seemingly damned soul, of which I had entirely lost track.

In the trial facility, they were forced to bind me with chains and a straitjacket. When I refused to sleep, muttering incantations to caffeinate my blood, they had to inject me with a sedative. Once the drugs took effect, and I was high and agreeable, the researchers led me through my ritual to summon a dream. It was all rather humiliating, but ultimately necessary.

As I drifted off—more like spinning, because of the drugs— my awareness was pulled yet again below the earth's crust. The sedative had put me at ease, and with the support of the researchers, I was able to regain control of my bird's eye view and stay hidden from the denizens of hell.

* * *

A young man wandered through a gray field, shrouded in roiling mists. He rubbed his arms, a vain attempt to subdue the incessant shivers caused by his soaked clothing and his overwhelming fever. His boots had been reduced to tatters, his toes bloodied from the long walk from the distant shore.

The man screamed his brother's name. He wondered how many hours—days?—he had been calling, searching to no avail. Now his voice was failing him, overused and wracked by pestilence.

The mist parted behind the man.

A devil had been stalking him for the better part of an hour and now moved in for its coveted feast. The man had no idea how much danger he was in, his awareness eroded by the gaseous influence of the mist which plagued the Screaming Fields, designed to disorient lost souls until they were eaten. I wondered why my dreams had bonded with someone so insignificant. But I watched on, as I have long since learned to trust my Art.

The devil, in an act of playful curiosity, revealed itself to the young man, who, in frenzied sublimation, soiled his already soiled trousers and fell weeping to his knees. It leaned forward on thick arms, hunching like a gorilla to support its bulbous torso, hanging its mottled face above the poor man's head, laughing at its good fortune and drooling with hunger.

"Please…" the man sobbed. "I need to find my brother. Let me find him, then you can eat me! You can eat me a million times over… Please…"

The great devil threw back its head and let out an incredulous guffaw, a terrible tumult of lost souls it had already devoured through the eons. What wonderful luck! It bent down low to the man's height, stitching together an agreeable countenance.

"You make a compelling proposition, poor mortal," said the devil. "Tell me, what is your brother's name?"

"Isshiah... He's just a boy..."

The devil hooted and snorted in amusement.

How foolish mortals can be! I need not remind you, dear reader, never tell a devil anyone's true name for any reason.

"Ah, yes... Isshiah... A wonderful name, a godly name. I can lead you to your Isshiah—on one condition."

Flesh folded in on itself in the beast's chest, and a scrawny set of hands emerged holding a scrap of papyrus, every inch covered with a scrawl of unintelligible script. It plucked a thick hair from the perimeter of its puffy areola and used it to circle a blank line with its inky blood.

The denizens of hell often revel in bureaucracy, and it is oft said that our modern governing structures were first employed in the Burning City of Grahtzildahn. Devils revel in the hunt— and when they catch their prey, they use contracts and riddles to play with their food like mouser cats chasing chipmunks up trees.

The man took hold of the improvised quill with a tremulous, battered hand. He was about to sign the devil's document, but was stopped by a shrill cry from above. Morgana's riders—her remaining Chosen mounted atop their griffins, emerged through the clouds in V-formation.

The woman taking point soared over the beast's head while the two men in the rear crashed into the demon, forcing it onto its back.

Syr Gabriel leapt from his mount and buried the head of his halberd into the devil's exposed, fleshy underbelly.

Dame Citha screamed a command, her griffin rearing back, allowing updrafts to carry it toward the clouds. She pulled the string of her longbow, a bolt of light appearing in an arrow's stead, then sent it spearing through the devil's skull—ending its miserable existence in an instant.

The young man fell onto his haunches before the riders, relief spreading across his haggard face. Syr Derrida dismounted, pulling the man to his feet.

"It ain't Arthur." Gabriel said, then spat on the ground.

Derrida sighed. "Clearly."

"Gut 'im and move on, eh?"

Terror flooded the man's expression, but Derrida raised a pacifying hand. "Don't you see who this is? Raise a finger and I'll feed it to Krakow." Derrida's mount snapped his beak to punctuate the point.

Still flying overwatch in the sky, Citha called out: "Time to move—the hordes caught our scent!"

"Tell me, boy," Derrida yanked the young man's arm and slapped him across the face, "have you seen Arthur?"

"Isshiah…" he groaned. "I'm searching for Isshiah… Father, please. You must help me."

"I don't give two shits about your simpering whelp, Derrida!" Gabriel roared over the thundering footfalls of the encroaching mass. "We need to fly!"

"Seth! Have you seen him?"

"Leave the boy, he's dead anyhow!"

"Don't leave me…" Seth bawled, collapsing at the feet of his ambivalent father.

"Derrida!" Citha yelled from on high, hurling beams of light at the drones leading the way for their heavier cohorts—all hungry for mortal flesh. "Time's up!"

Syr Derrida took a final glance at the scared little boy before him. He had never cared for Seth; he had always been a weakling. A pathetic excuse for an heir… and just when his eldest son was beginning to show promise, he had committed the most cowardly act of all, betraying their entire family in one fell swoop.

What enraged Derrida most was how much Seth reminded him of himself. Derrida had never been brave—he was a pragmatist, only choosing battles he knew he could win. Yet his shit of a son had made it halfway across the Screaming Fields unarmed and unmounted as his failing body ate itself. Could Derrida have done the same?

Probably not.

"On your feet, lad!" Derrida mounted and pulled Seth onto Krakow's back. A mental command brought them sweeping into the sky just as the skittering waves closed in, trampling over themselves in a blood-starved frenzy.

Gabriel glared at Derrida as they continued to the threshold, the border between Morgana's realm and Grahtzildahn. Morgana's newest Herald cared not for his companion's resentment—he did not intend for the lumbering fool to return.

IV

"And now you've seen," Ibrahim whispered, rubbing Kateryna's back tenderly. "So, I shall recite all you need to know."

The old man raised his arms, throwing his head back as he chanted in a strange tongue Kateryna could not comprehend.

The lantern swung like a pendulum, back and forth, thick plumes of smoke weeping between the panes of wavy glass, sinking to hover just above the floor.

Kateryna fell back onto her hands when she looked into Ibrahim's eyes, glowing perfect white. He rose, standing over her, possessed by a grotesque dance twisting and contorting his limbs, fingers weaving unknowable forces into the tapestry of prophesy.

"The Great Stair stands in the center of the Burning City— it leads all the way up… and all the way down. Salvation one way, damnation, the other!

"Your mother is rooted in the riverbed parting the shores of Life and Death, the Dusk and the Dawn. If you wish to find her, you must ascend the Stair. To survive, you must let go of the pain in your heart, all of it, for your soul will soon face overwhelming assault."

Kateryna nodded and wiped a tear from her eye. "I understand what I need to do."

"Good, child." Ibrahim sighed, an eldritch wind escaping his lungs. "Good."

The old man closed his eyes, releasing the incantation with a pulse of air that dispersed the lingering smoke. He redressed the soiled linens around his face, then turned towards Cain.

"I do not have a prophesy for you," Ibrahim said. "Yet my matron bid I deliver you a message. If you'll hear it."

Cain blanched, the deep lines of his face carved into a dreadful mask. "I will hear it."

Surrounding shadows closed in, threatening to snuff out what meager light remained. A chill skittered across Kateryna's neck as the walls expanded, and the hut itself breathed in—then back out.

"Your role is not so simple," the old man said, annunciating each word in a rehearsed mimicry of the Valentine accent. "You stand at a crossroads, and you must tread the mire to make the final push. Retrieve the blade forged from the blood of a thousand heretics. Thrust its point into the heart of evil. Only then can Life and Death walk together again."

"These are not your words…"

"No." Ibrahim's expression softened. "They are not. Take them as you will—but consider them with care."

"I cannot—"

"You've stricken this world with imbalance!" The old man's voice shook the walls, rattling the bamboo chimes lining the ceiling. "Surely, you can muster the courage to correct it!"

Montauk's tocsin cry sounded from outside. Cain leapt to his feet and charged through the invisible doorway, light blooming into an elongated door-shaped hole in the shadows.

Kateryna scrambled to follow, but Ibrahim held her wrist, beckoning her to wait. "Dear Kateryna Cain of Undton, take these gifts to assist your journey. You need not charge into the abyss empty-handed."

He handed her a leather kidney bag decorated with dark beaded cords. "This contains three doses of my elixir. It is all I have to give; take care to ration it."

The old man then held out his hands, drawing a plain iron-tipped spear from thin air. "This is the Sun Spear of Dawn. May it light your way and always return to you."

The spear was lighter than Kateryna's lost harpoon but felt more durable. The haft was hewn from the branch of a sycamore, sanded and polished to a smooth matte finish. It hardly looked like a divine artifact—but a spear was a spear, and it was more than she had before.

Balance and chaos.

"Thank you, Ibrahim…"

"Now go!"

Kateryna dashed after Cain. He stood at the edge of the porch, sword in hand, Montauk crouching low beside him. Three riders, clad in the same black armor as Cain and mounted atop their own monsters, hovered around the hut. She gasped when she saw the hostage on the back of the smallest griffin.

"Seth!"

Cain held her behind him with his off hand. She caught a glimpse of the towering drop just over the ledge and immediately felt her stomach lurch. Seth locked eyes with her, but the gaunt rider had clamped a gloved hand over his mouth.

"Give it up, Arthur!" the gaunt man said. "This doesn't have to get ugly. Let us do our jobs, eh? You can finally have some much-needed rest…"

"Get onto Montauk," Cain whispered to Kateryna. "Fly to the Burning City."

Kateryna shook her head. "I'm not leaving without you—you're coming with me."

"Ain't no chance of that, girl," said a hulking rider. "Your old man's screams are about to join the rest in the Fields."

"Kat," Cain said, glaring at the three riders. "Go."

Seth ripped the gaunt man's hand from his mouth. "She has nothing to do with this!"

The gaunt man sighed. "If we let your girl go, will you let us get this over with?"

"Yes."

"Foolish," said the third rider, a Skanu woman with a shaved head, her face adorned with silver jewelry. "The girl will return."

"Way I see it," the gaunt man said, unsheathing his sword, "the Goddess demanded Arthur's head—so that's all we'll take."

"Coward," said the big man.

"Enough!" Cain stepped off the porch into open air, as if it were solid ground.

Bright light shone through his pores, through his eyes and mouth—quickly shadowed by the unfurling of a great raven's wings. Cain's body contorted, his skin bubbling and roiling like so many beetles burrowing into a corpse, then shimmering as a diamond in the glow of morning.

The aspect of a tall, full-bodied woman encompassed Cain's withered form—a Valkyrie of Wystran myth, straight out of the stories Kateryna's mother had told her as a girl.

"Declared for death or no," the Valkyrie's voice resounded through the air. Storm clouds gathered above, rolling and toppling over one another. Lightning flashed and thunder clapped in time with the beat of the Valkyrie's wings. "I am still the Chosen, the living avatar of the Great Mother's divine will. If you should take my vessel, do not expect me to stand idle."

The Valkyrie raised Cain's battered longsword, now wreathed in a shroud of holy flame.

The two men exchanged incredulous glances. The Skanu lowered her head in rushed prayer. Kateryna fell back into Montauk.

"This doesn't make sense," the gaunt man muttered. "Who is she?"

"The Goddess lives, Derrida!" the Skanu cried. "As she once was, the Goddess lives!"

"I'm bored of this farce," the big man hefted his halberd over his shoulder. "I yearn for blood!"

Montauk scooped her head between Kateryna's legs, tossing her into Cain's saddle, and launched into the sky and away from the coming battle. The wind battering Kateryna's face, she leaned into Montauk's ebon feathers for succor against the forces of gravity she was not accustomed to. Kateryna yanked on the beast's feathers, screaming for it to halt, but Cain's beloved griffin paid no heed.

Kateryna's heart skipped a beat as she watched her father— no, the Valkyrie, the Goddess Incarnate—charge the big man, who twisted, narrowly evading the killing thrust of her flaming sword. The other two riders dipped, repositioning into a defensive formation. In the chaos of the maneuver, Seth had slipped from the gaunt man's saddle, plummeting towards the waves below.

"Montauk! Please!" Kateryna screamed, tears flowing down her face. She was powerless, forced to watch her beloved die. Again.

Because I am weak—because I am cursed to fail him, over and over.

A soothing voice billowed through her mind, clear as a mother's whisper to her babe. *"You are not powerless, dear Kateryna."*

Montauk?

"Cain does not speak. Nor should you."

Dive, Montauk. Please.

"As you wish."

V

From the collected journals of a mad wizard

For seven nights, I dreamt beneath the observation of Citadel scholars, researchers dedicated to decoding the *discipline* of oneiromancy. Fools! When will they realize that sorcery is art, not science—I've always said: Phrygian Sorcery is beholden to the laws of science but remains entirely subjective in its application.

I must admit, I was humiliated. There I was, one of the four founding archmagi—my teachings informed sorcerous study and arcane theory for generations—confined to a padded room with only a one-way viewing window for company.

I resisted the orderlies tooth and nail. They dressed me in a scratchy gown, leaving my posterior exposed to the air. They bound my arms and legs with dampening chains to prevent the use of my Art to crush them like so many bugs. I ate only when coerced. And they beset me with fruitless sponge baths when I at last grew too tired to resist.

By the third night, my visions had become so vivid, so disturbing, that my body convulsed in wild fits—eventually, they had to lash me to the bed, as I began to float snoozing to the ceiling.

I later read reports claiming that I was muttering incoherently through waking hours and slumber alike. This was not nonsense, dear reader, for I recited the words of hell;

conversations I overheard in Morgana's Hall, in the Demon King Grahtz's court. I bleated like a nightmare and screeched like a lemure, my soul ablaze with hellfire.

My symptoms lessened by the final night of my internment. My dreams returned to those unwitting friends: the wicked Syr Arthur Cain and my sweet Kateryna.

* * *

Cain wore the aspect of Dusk, the last vestige of the Goddess as she had been. Such a thing should have been impossible, but in the Dread Angel's hubris, her blind obsession for her Chosen, she had failed to recognize a lingering spark in his heart—a spark that had once belonged to her.

For decades, Citadel scholars argued the merit of eye-witness accounts claiming an angel laid waste to Idraan, finally chasing the Kaza'dur back to whence they came. Now I saw the truth for myself—ashamed, too, as my doubts of such accounts had cost people their lives.

Dusk's Avatar charged Syr Derrida first. Being the weakest fighter, he was an easy target—and he carried a passenger, besides. Dusk's newly named Herald drove his white-faced griffin low, spinning in the air to evade the wide arc of the angel's flaming sword.

Seth, unaccustomed to flight, fell from the saddle and plummeted towards the black waves below.

Kateryna dived after him, racing the poor boy to the sea. Holding the saddle horn with one hand, reaching into the open air with the other, Kateryna yanked Seth from his fall, pulling him by the hem of his tunic onto her lap.

With the battle raging above them, they fled for the shimmering threshold, to Grahtzildahn.

Dame Citha watched the pair fly away and, for an instant, considered sending an arrow for Montauk's heart. Gabriel rushed by overhead, returning her attention to the raging angel that so resembled Citha's beloved goddess—a version of her, at least, lost to time.

"Take the rear, strong right!" Gabriel shouted.

Citha dug her stirrups into Stockholm, who flapped his great wings until she fell in behind and above Gabriel. They surged through the air trailing Derrida's retreat. Soon, they cleared the sea, flying over the blackened coastline of the Screaming Fields.

From her view, Citha saw Derrida's evasion failing—he howled in pain as he parried a near-lethal blow from Dusk's avatar. The avatar's flaming sword showered sparks over him as Derrida batted it aside with his pitiful smallsword.

Divided loyalties and uncertainty clashed in her heart. Citha drew back her bowstring, an arrow of perfect light manifesting between her fingers.

"Forgive me, Goddess…"

Citha loosed her arrow, striking the avatar in the thigh. The blow did nothing but enrage her further.

Gabriel raised his halberd, poised to kill, for a center slash, but his blade sliced naught but air.

A shroud of darkness—no, a shadow—fell over Citha. She blinked, and Dusk was in front of her. Citha commanded Stockholm to lean forward so she could engage the avatar, but the griffin leaned backward instead, catching the avatar's flaming blade in Citha's place.

Always the stubborn prick, her poor Stockholm.

Gabriel circled back round, striking from above, leveraging the length of his halberd like an oar. He managed a shallow cut on the avatar's scalp but paid for it with her searing blade plunging through his mount's belly and into his ass.

Stockholm drifted, dying, to the ground.

Derrida, following close behind from Gabriel's leading left, struck the avatar's armored back. He cursed as the blade of his smallsword shattered against its divine armor.

Gabriel roared, consumed with battle-joy and bloodlust. His bleeding mount somehow remained airborne, still circling Dusk. Gabriel twisted his halberd for a passing back swing. Smiling wide, his teeth bared, he reveled in the glory this prey would bring. He imagined the head of his halberd buried in the angel's chest, cutting free her lungs.

Instead, it was his chest that was on fire—the avatar had shifted so Gabriel struck only adamant breastplate. In retaliation, the angel gripped his throat, plunging her blade into his heart.

"She isn't real..." Gabriel coughed, thick blood pooling in the corners of his small, pouting mouth. "None of this is real."

Gabriel, along with his massive mount, plunged into the black earth, a plume of dust exploding in their wake.

When the cloud cleared, Dusk's avatar landed to find Syr Derrida standing over Gabriel's corpse—the remains of his smallsword jutting out of the big man's face.

The angel raised her blade. Derrida sucked in a deep breath through clogged nostrils and fell to his knees.

"Please," he said. "I've had enough blood to last lifetimes."

The rage in the angel's eyes cooled; the roiling storm above slowed to a gentle drizzle as the flame of her sword extinguished. The Goddess Incarnate looked down upon her knight, moved by the regret painting his face.

"I thought you were gone," Derrida went on, "so I gave up hope. I see now I was wrong. Allow me to continue my service in Dusk's name..."

"I gave up, too," Cain and the angel said in unison. The avatar's form faded away. Cain, battered and wounded, fell into Derrida's arms. Dusk's voice, disembodied: "Take care of him, my knight. We are almost through this darkness."

Krakow cried out before Stockholm's limp form. Derrida eased Cain onto the ground and rushed over to Citha's side. She writhed beneath the dead weight of her fallen mount, her right leg crushed; her heart was beginning to slow, her boiling blood cooling to a simmer.

Derrida's eyes cast over her, then to Gabriel's bleeding corpse. "He was always a bloody pain, wasn't he?"

Citha pulled vainly at her leg, then let out an ululating scream.

"You saw the Goddess…" Derrida rubbed his temples, knelt before Citha. "We all saw her."

Breathless, she said: "Yes."

"As she was before. She was whole."

"…Yes."

"What do we do?"

Citha's eyes rolled to Cain, unconscious on the ground. "You need to take him… protect him."

Derrida laughed, shaking his head. "I'm bloody useless! I can't do this alone—I can't leave you."

"You must." Citha grimaced as a sharp pain shot from her heel through the sack of meat that had once been her leg.

With those final words, Derrida retrieved his blade from Gabriel's skull. The weapon had always seemed to make its way back to him for better or worse. But its time had ended—his smallsword had always been better suited for fencing with children than for warfare, for committing heresies across a generation or more.

Derrida tested the balance of the broken blade. After all these years, holding the thing for too long still made his wrist ache, ever the epitome of inadequacy. But now, everything rested upon his shoulders.

"Do you wish to rest, Citha?" Derrida said, squeezing his watering eyes shut.

"I'm not ready for that," she gasped. "Free me, and I'll make my own way. I'll be of no help to you like this."

"Morgana might find you."

Citha's mouth fell flat. "With what we saw... I'll take that risk.

Derrida tightened his grip on his sword, shivers rolling down his spine. "Okay, then."

FOUR

Let me tell you, boy
a tale of down below.
Where the days are hard
and the beds are stone.

I'll tell you the tale
of when time had split.
And the fires of hell
were our only light.

Ephraim (-54 to 47)
"Down Below," published Year 40.

I

In the sky, crossing the threshold

Grahtzildahn, second layer of Pandemonium

The dreamlike threshold separating the unceasing storms of the Vale Betwixt shimmered with the furnace heat of Grahtzildahn. The nearer they drew, the sorcerous wall appeared more like an illusion than something material. The barrier danced, milky tendrils jittering through translucent skin like living fibers of an onion stalk. As Montauk slowly ascended the wall's height, preparing for a steep dive to pierce its membrane, Kateryna began to feel wisps of hot wind cutting across her face and hands.

Kateryna held fast to the saddle horn with one hand, brandishing the Sun Spear of Dawn with the other as Seth clutched to her waist. Her stomach lurched as Montauk withdrew her wings and plunged into the barrier.

Like flies stuck in amber, their velocity was extinguished by the grasping tendrils, coated with sticky, sorcerous bile. Oily fingers clasped Montauk's legs, holding her fast. Searching hands fondled Kateryna, creeping up her shins, then her thighs. She clenched her abdomen, her hamstrings, locking herself into the saddle against the wall's festering will.

Seth slid back, pulled away. Kateryna released the saddle horn, catching his wrist. His face contorted, reflected pain, but his scream was inaudible. She gasped for air—but the space inside the wall was naught but void. Montauk pawed helplessly for freedom, her massive heart pounding, starving for oxygen.

Thump, thump. Thump, thump.

Kateryna struggled against the weight of worlds to lift Dawn's spear. The iron tip cut slowly through the malaise— then, ignited with radiant flame. The tendrils shriveled from the blinding light. A hole burned into the wall's viscous skin, allowing scorched air to fill the space, exploding with holy flame around Montauk.

The griffin bucked and flapped her great wings. Back in open air, the torrid updrafts carried them to the freedom of the skies over Grahtzildahn. They had crossed the threshold between hells. The stench of moldering earth of the Screaming Fields fled for that of blackened plains beyond—sulfur and smoldering hair; the tepid humidity of the Vale Betwixt evaporated for the arid furnace that was Grahtzildahn.

Kateryna's vision wavered, collapsing around the periphery.

"Rest now, young ones," Montauk said. *"You need time to acclimate to this place. I will find us shelter."*

Thank you, Montauk... Kateryna thought as sleep claimed her.

* * *

Beneath the surface of the badlands

Grahtzildahn, second layer of Pandemonium

Kateryna woke, bundled between Seth and Montauk. It was dark, and the stagnant air was cool and musty. Bulbous stalagmites depended from the ceiling, denticulate ripples running along their lengths. Some had reached all the way to the ground, forming knobby pillars.

Off in the distance, she heard a gentle drip falling into a larger body of water.

Her mouth was dry, her lips splitting at the seams, her body drenched with clinging sweat. She rose, stripping off everything she wore, save for her boots and small clothes. Arms raised to touch the rough stone ceiling above, she stretched out the lingering pain that came with a perilous journey.

She looked down at Seth, yet consumed by a fitful sleep, choking on bile with every belabored breath. Dark blemishes scored the surface of his skin. Kateryna knew they would soon burst into the token black boils, weeping fetid pus, inviting further infection, marking the final stages of Morgana's pestilence.

Kneeling, she nudged him awake. Seth was slow to emerge from his stupor, his eyes opening before rolling back again. Finally, he was overtaken by a coughing fit. Kateryna lifted him upright, pounding his back and holding his hand as he vomited blood and bile.

"Kat…" He panted, breathless. "Where are we?"

"I don't know—underground. There's water further down, but I don't want to go alone."

"I can't…" His eyes returned to his rancid spew, seeping into the parched rock of the cave floor. "It won't be long, now. We both know how this ends."

"Nonsense." Kateryna picked up her satchel, reached inside. Her fingers glanced across the cold glass. "Open wide."

"Why? I'd rather not play doctor—"

Too exhausted to explain, Kateryna pulled out one of the three vials Ibrahim had given her. Pulling off the cork, she grabbed a handful of Seth's sandy hair, forced his head back, and dumped the bright elixir down his gullet. She watched in awe as the inflamed sores lining his throat calmed, then receded to mere bumps.

Seth doubled over, coughing again, but soon quieted as the elixir did its work. He breathed deep and laughed. "Gods in hell! That's… I feel—I don't know! I can't remember the last time I've felt healthy."

"It's temporary. It suppresses the symptoms, but the disease lives on." She took a pull of a second flask. "I have only one more dose, so we'll need to keep moving as soon as Montauk has recovered. Do you have a weapon?"

Seth looked down at his moccasins. "I don't..."

"Seth!"

"What?"

"How have you survived?"

"Ain't like I'd have a chance in combat, anyway!" Seth sighed. "Besides, if it weren't for the riders, I wouldn't have made it."

Derrida saved him? The Dread Angel's grip must be weakening across the board... Not just with me and Cain.

Montauk opened her eyes as they spoke. The griffin rose and stretched, arching her back. Her voice flowed within Kateryna's consciousness as a gentle breeze. *"Check my saddle, young one. Cain always stows a sidearm."*

Seth stared at Kateryna. She nodded. Seth approached Montauk and sifted through her saddlebags. He drew a silver flanged mace.

"Least I'll get to hit something, before I die again..."

Fortunately, there was nothing awaiting them further down the cave, only soothing, cool air—a rarity, to be sure, as Kateryna already knew from her seconds of consciousness in the dry heat of the surface.

They came upon a narrow passage; they could freely move their arms and upper bodies, but two shelves closed in at waist height, and all they could do was sidle along. Progress through the tortuous path was slow and painful, as fingers of jagged rock clawed at their flesh. The dripping knell had risen from a tinkling to a clangorous din, and after a half hour, they at last emerged from the gantlet into a cavern, finding an underground spring resting at its center.

The spring was the size of a large bathtub, like the one Kateryna's mother once enjoyed in her first life. A stalactite the size of a pinky finger was the source of the drippage, supplying the spring's reservoir, one drop at a time, over the course of eons.

Seth ambled past her and buried his face in the pool. He only came up for air once he had drunk enough to satiate the thirst of the entirety of Monrovia.

"I've never known such bliss," Seth said, collapsing on his back. "I could stay here forever."

It was a tempting prospect. They might have been able to manage it, too, subsisting on cave mushrooms and rat meat. But the pestilence had already fixed a time and date for their impending doom. Or, before that, some hellish beast might wander in for a drink.

If not one death, then another.

Kateryna knelt beside him, drank from her cupped hands. The water was warm and mineral-rich. A bit acrid, stale. But it was water. Clean, clear water. She assumed such blessings dissolved long ago.

"Seth?" Kateryna ventured. A vision lingered in her mind's eye; a memory of standing on those golden hills; her back turned away from home, a ring in her palm.

"Yeah?"

"Do you remember... what I did to you?"

At first, his expression was questioning, oblivious. Then, understanding spread across his face, soon replaced by a flash of pain settling into grim acceptance.

"I do, now." He shook his head. "I haven't thought about that in ages."

"Neither have I. I've only just remembered."

"It's this place, isn't it?"

"The fog... it was *her* doing." Kateryna swung about, looked Seth in the eyes; they were sallow, bloodshot. He only nodded, his glare cold as the stone walls surrounding them. "I'm so sorry, Seth." She began to sob, "I'm so..."

He scoffed, flung a dismissive hand. "That's far away now. Long in the past."

"No, it isn't."

"No..." He sighed. "It isn't."

"Did you..." She looked away, unable to look him in the eye, for what she next needed to ask. "Did you do it—because of me?"

Memories danced across his features, behind his tortured eyes. Before her, Seth relived a lifetime of trauma and pain, from which death should have long since freed his weary soul.

Seth heaved, tears streaming down his battered cheeks. "Kat... You were everything to me. And then you—"

"I did."

"Why?" He shook his head repeatedly. "Why, Kat? Did you not love me?"

"Of course I did—"

"Then why did you leave?" Seth shouted, his knuckles white as he gripped the shaft of Cain's mace.

"I didn't know..." Kateryna stammered, tears obscuring her vision, stealing her breath. "I just—"

"You just what?" He rose, dropping the mace clattering upon the hard ground. "Please, tell me why you left!"

"I loved—still love you," she said, as memories of her old life flooded back into her mind. "But I knew... I was afraid I wasn't the woman you needed by your side. I'm so..."

"Kat," Seth said, his heaving chest deflating as the breath of anger seeped from lungs punctured by disease, and a heart riven by grief. "Did you think I wanted you to change?"

She stared at him. Never had Kateryna bothered to ask herself that question, only presumed what others might have thought of her—of them. The Valentine aristocracy was an orthodox bunch, full of gossips and self-styled judges of what is good and proper. She had always existed on the fringes of those circles for the way she looked, for the way she acted... for who she was. *A Wystran, a scoundrel, a ruffian, a fisher, a baker, a ranger, a sailor. In other words—not a real woman.*

Her lower lip quivered. She was torn open, her innards splayed out in front of him. *Has it been so simple, this whole time?*

"I don't know."

Seth enfolded her in his warm embrace. He had become so thin and frail, he nearly crumpled beneath her strength as she returned the gesture.

Kateryna buried her face in the space between his shoulder and his neck, her hot tears cutting a path through the grime coating his copper flesh.

Words have power. Kateryna knew this. The power to maim, to wound—but rarely to mend. So, they held each other in silence for what felt like years. Perhaps years had indeed passed around them. She kissed him on the cheek. He looked into her eyes, taking in her entire being, and kissed her lips, just as he had all those summers ago in the golden wheat fields, on the borders between their fathers' holdings, their castles standing vigil at their backs.

They undressed, beholding each other as they were: beaten, bruised, blemished with blackened boils that beat in time with their broken hearts. The filth of hell clung to them. They had languished in it for so long.

And why?

For the sin of being born human.

Gods save the proud.

Immersed in the warm water of the spring—a miracle in its own right, in a place where miracles stilled in the womb—they held each other for fear of losing the precious memories they had only just reclaimed.

The waters lapped gently between Kateryna's breasts, pooled in Seth's dense chest hair. Staring into each other's eyes, never once looking away, she wrapped her legs around his waist, and together they swayed, washing away years of detritus.

And so much pain.

* * *

In the sky, approaching the Burning City

Grahtzildahn, second layer of Pandemonium

Arid winds buffeted Kateryna's face; infinitesimal particulates opened invisible abrasions over every inch of her exposed skin. Below, the land was red, iron-rich dirt covering the craggy, boundless expanse. Towers of lavender flames ruptured the landscape, geysers fueled by boiling springs, much hotter than the one they had found deep beneath the surface.

She saw the Great Stair in the distance. It climbed from the horizon to the hard ceiling, leagues high. A jagged cityscape surrounded it, a shimmering mirage refracting scintillant torchlight in all directions. Brass walls surrounded leaning spires of blackened stone, climbing impossible slopes as if the city were one of the great mountains overlooking Valencia, filling its belly in preparation to erupt its vengeance upon the flat plains beyond.

The Burning City…

There was lurid beauty to the spectacle, despite the sinister reality of Pandemonium. *Is it our nature that coerces us into seeing the good within a structure built with evil intent? Or does there remain a glimmer of hope, even in the most downtrodden reaches of existence?*

A shrieking din assaulted her ears. Seth groaned, clutching his head. Montauk whinnied and began a rapid descent.

Men shouted below. Red and brown figures scrambled on the ground, their armor glittering from the flaming geysers surrounding them. A deep horn bellowed from the city, signaling the emergence of a great winged reptilian creature from its nest in the ceiling above.

"Duck!" Kateryna yelled as she pressed herself into the griffin's mane.

A swarm of arrows launched from the masses below. Montauk spun, flourishing her wings, batting away the whistling shafts. Kateryna lifted the Sun Spear of Dawn overhead, unsure what good it would do, but trusting in the Oracle's promise.

May you light my way!

The wyrm screeched over their heads, swooped low, and twisted in the air before appearing in front of them to block Montauk's flight. The beast was gaunt, clearly starving. Its ruby scales clicked and popped, as if skittering insects commanded its movements, rather than blood and sinew.

An orb of light burst from the Sun Spear, suffusing furnace heat with divine warmth. The wyrm shriveled back, screeching as it fell behind Montauk. The weapon's shaft vibrated in her hand with vigor—with life. Kateryna was no longer so alone, so forgotten; someone watched on from above, lending a helping hand. *There might be hope yet.*

Still—the path to the Great Stair remained fraught with many perils.

"*Worry not, young one,*" Montauk whispered. "*I've lived long. I've lived well. I will deliver you no matter the cost!*"

Another shriek shook the ceiling above, the very air, shattering Dawn's protective light, shards of morning raining death on the hapless foot soldiers below. The wyrm's shadow passed over them, an infernal gust nearly blowing Kateryna and Seth off Montauk's back. The wyrm, once a great dragon of old, yearning to reclaim its superiority over the skies, twisted around and matched Montauk's speed.

Kateryna reversed her grip on the spear, raised it above her shoulder, and poised to throw. She thanked the gods for Cain's insistence that she learn how to use such a weapon, despite the outrage of his aristocratic colleagues. The spear grew hot, the tip glowing bright orange.

The wyrm furled its great wings, diving in again to block Montauk's path, molten rage boiling within its rubrous maw.

Kateryna hurled the Sun Spear of Dawn, which turned to a bolt of lightning as it arced from her hand. The bolt tore a gaping wound in the thin membrane of the wyrm's wing, and it plummeted, screaming to the fields below, where its weight exploded into the ground, destroying the ranks of soldiers pursuing them.

The Burning City drew near. Brass rooftops glinted in Kateryna's periphery. Blackened stone structures leaned wearily upon molten bases, warped and withered under centuries of infernal heat uncounted. The people damned to live in the streets screamed and panicked at the sight of Montauk, a black mass of wings, completely alien to them in the fiery realm of the Demon King Grahtz.

"I've taken you as far as I can, young one."

We're nearly there! Don't give up, Montauk!

A mechanical crack thundered from a tower set within the palace's outer wall. Something slammed into Montauk, knocking her from the air and careening towards the wall. Kateryna's heart lurched as she realized what Montauk had meant.

No!

In the instant before impact, Kateryna held out her hand in vain hopes the Sun Spear might reappear, or that she might cast some ancient eldritch spell that would save them—but she had thrown the spear, and she was out of options.

"Hold tight…" Montauk's labored thoughts trudged into her mind. *"I will protect you!"* The great griffin crashed through the

parapet, bringing down slabs of shattered stone as they burst into the courtyard, flattening scattering servants and bystanders who fled too late.

Kateryna coiled her fingers in Montauk's feathered mane, hugging her tight as she thrashed about. Montauk's flight skidded to a final halt, and Kateryna felt the griffin's powerful heart cease to beat.

Thump, thump. Thump...

II

From the collected journals of a mad wizard

When next I dreamt of Pandemonium, I was caught in the grasping tar of the Wall of Souls between Grahtzildahn and the Vale Betwixt. My influence was suspended, entirely stunted, a lingering side-effect of having witnessed the beautiful aspect of Dusk.

You must understand, dear reader, that the gods are complex in their physical manifestations. Their presence on Earth—or in Hell, beneath the Earth's crust—is not indicative of truth. Rather, such beings undergo a process of *visuospatial translation* to be interpreted by the mortal eye, bound by the limitations of the material world.

A fragment of Morgana existed within Cain, her chosen champion in life and in death. Dusk, which is how I will refer to this fragmented aspect hence, is an echo of her previous incarnation as the benevolent shepherd of lost souls into the Great Beyond. This is to say, her power—Cain's power—is overwhelming, especially within the proximity of her corrupted whole.

My observers—jailers, in truth—grew displeased with my prolonged impotence. At first, they accused me of withholding my prophetic visions out of spite. My dear friend, Headmaster Pascal Doon, knew better. He understood that I yearned above all else to witness myth in the making. He understood the gravity of the strange happenings unfolding beneath our feet.

It was four more days of rigorous nothing before my observers lost interest in my flaccid sorcery, and finally granted me a night of much needed privacy. That same night, my friend appeared in my quarters—my cell—with a bedroll in hand. "I will dream with you," Pascal Doon said. "It's clear this situation is growing beyond our collective ken. Should anything untoward come to pass, I am with you."

I had no words in reply to this magnanimous gesture. Surely, my friend saw the significance it had on me as I shed a single tear from my obsolescent eye.

"Shall we begin?" he asked at length.

"Like old times, eh?"

Pascal Doon chuckled. "This time, we aren't searching for maidens bathing in rivers."

"No. Instead, we search for goddesses with the power to rend lost souls asunder."

"True enough, friend. True enough."

The headmaster laid out his bedroll, and together we chanted our incantations to summon sleep, to conjure a dream. My eyes fluttered shut. Through our combined powers, when I opened them again, I was standing inside the court of the Demon King Grahtz.

* * *

I stood at attention on a polished marble floor of diamond-shaped tiles, refracting swirls of cream in black tea, suffused with the warm glow of the hanging braziers above. I took in a measured breath—about six seconds to fill all three of my lungs with piquant air—and prepared myself to face my lord.

Today held particular significance for me—I was to be named a legionnaire of the Reborn Legion, sworn to defend my city from those hellish invaders seeking to destroy our hard-fought order. Each lost soul in the generous Lord Grahtz's court dreams of being the subject of this ceremony, of the cool steel of his sword to be placed gently on their shoulders.

He called my name—my old name. I marched down the
aisle to the throne and kneeled before the lord.

The Great Lord Grahtz had ruled the Burning City
of Grahtzildahn, against all odds, for ten thousand years,
protecting the Great Stair from the fell beasts yearning to feast
upon the mortal flesh above. I was fortunate to awaken under
the good lord's care, within those glorious walls, of all places.
My comrades had told me tales of their previous lives in the
deeper layers of Pandemonium. The officer who trained me,
who groomed me for the station I was about to attain, told
me that she had existed as a sack of living flesh for nearly five
hundred years before she found a ledge high enough to end her
misery. She woke in Grahtzildahn, reborn.

Indeed, I was fortunate in myriad ways—I had lived only
on the first layer, suspended above the Congealed Sea for a mere
half century. When first I awoke in my new form, metallic and
inorganic, I was deeply disturbed. This is normal for the souls
captured by the lord's recruiters; it takes time for the natural
soul to acclimate to the confines of a cold, unfeeling body.
Though my shell was at first empty, I trained and honed my
skills, and over time flesh grew within; an organism to nurture
my soul, as my shell protects it.

Today, I woke with a beating heart, and so Lord Grahtz sent
his summons. I would be inducted before the entirety of my
community, my family.

My lord sat leisurely upon his throne, smiling down
unto me. He was like us once, a lost soul. But it was his self-
sacrifice that made our glorious rebirth as his soldiers possible.
As I kneeled, he laid his blade clinking serenely on my right
shoulder, then my left.

"Rise, my son," said the lord, his voice a cerulean waterfall
wetting the sharp edges of the court. "You have proven thyself
worthy. You have grown… and thus, you will live."

"Thank you…" I croaked, unable to conjure more worthy
words fit for my divine benefactor. For the first time, I looked
up from my toes—sabatons forged in the shape of toes—and

beheld his visage. The face of the Great Lord Grahtz, eternal ruler of the Burning City of Grahtzildahn, is a grotesque sight for those who do not understand him. To craft his legion, he first had to learn, to suffer, through many trials and many more errors. His own flesh, mottled and mutated, overgrew the armor he had forged for himself before his ascension. Now, he is bound to his throne, tormented with constant agonies so that my kind may live.

"Once a boy, cursed to remain so for all eternity," said the good lord, "you have been remade into a man, forged of silver, brass, and obsidian. You are now whole—I name you *Invictus,* for your unwavering courage!"

"I am your humble servant, my lord."

A glimmer of a grin danced across his twisted countenance. He had opened his mouth to speak when the throne room's doors crashed open behind me, and a frenzied legionnaire sprinted toward the throne.

"What is the meaning of this interruption?" Grahtz snarled.

"The walls are breached, my lord!" the intruder cried.

"Breached? Impossible!"

"The Dread Angel attacks, sire! A dark creature of her brood was flying for the Stair, but we shot it down. We've captured its riders."

Lord Grahtz's fury cooled to simmering contemplation, then flashed to concern. "Invictus!"

"Yes, lord?"

"Take the Dread Angel's riders into the Pit. Learn what they're after. This is your first command, as one of my Reborn."

"It shall be done."

* * *

We woke with a start. I was drenched in sweat, and my dear draconian friend would have been, too, if he possessed the glands. It is a well-known limitation of oneiromancy that one must first visit in the waking world the places he wishes to surveil before he can dream of them. I had scoured Morgana's realm, spent years of my life among the sickly people of Monrovia. And I tell you, dear reader, that I have never set one foot onto the arid plains of Grahtzildahn, nor into the limits of the Burning City.

"Headmaster..." I panted and took a deep pull from the cup on my bedside table. "Did *you* take us into the second layer?"

Pascal Doon sighed wearily as he rose and began to pace. "I did not. In all my eons, I have yet to gather the gumption to traverse the underworld. You are uniquely tenacious in that way, my friend."

"What does it mean, to inhabit such a creature against our combined wills?"

"It means that we must return to sleep, post haste! I see now that your obsession is warranted. We witness uncanny events."

Comforted by the much-needed validation from my closest, oldest friend, I eased back into my cot, desiring the comfort of my silken mattress back in my quarters. I took three deep breaths, then chanted my incantation anew. Pascal Doon joined, and soon, the room spun around us, fading from reality.

III

A conversation, somewhere far away.

Are you beginning to catch those fleeting memories, flashing like torch bugs in the back of your mind? Yes—I can see that you are. You've seen it all: a life, a death, and everything in between.

Shall I continue?

Good. Time is short, and there is one more story you must hear before you embark on this final journey...

You had spent decades of your life warring in the name of Valencia against the Kaza'dur. I need not remind you of their menace, of their ruthless sapping of our sweet world, stealing all it has to give. You fought bravely in a dozen battles, reclaimed the southern outlands, and established the borders we appreciate today. But the Kaza'duran influence—now, Idraani culture—was potent, contagious.

Invaders or no, the snakes assimilated the people beneath them.

The thirst for greatness, for conquest—in business and war, besides—was insatiable. High King Laszlo Balderas hungered to make his own mark upon the world.

By royal decree, yourself, Syr Gabriel, Dame Citha, and Syr Derrida left your homes, leading a host of one hundred thousand soldiers to brave the sands. The faith of your comrades waned with the changing times; they were not in conversation with the Goddess as you were. Dusk remained a gentle presence in your mind. Yet you had no way of knowing that her presence was unravelling from the fabric of your heart, a dark influence slowly erasing her.

Three years it took to cross the Endless Sands.

You lost countless soldiers to starvation, heat stroke, and the venom of scorpions and serpents alike. So too, enemy lances— the Kaza'dur were beastly foes, hiding beneath the sands, ambushing your caravans at every crossing. They killed brutally, indiscriminately, the wounded and refugees; men, women, children, and elders—blood was blood, and nothing to them tasted better than human blood.

Still, you marched ever onward through their unearthly domain to make right a world off kilter. The soldiers stayed close, never straying far from their trains. When men ambled off in search of privacy to release a long stream of brown piss, the snakes emerged, swallowing them whole, or breaking their minds to use against your forces as thoughtless drones.

And yet you arrived at the gates of Idraan, the city of another world. Three years' march, and sixty thousand souls lost.

"No matter!" you had said to Derrida one night. "Dusk will shepherd them home."

By the seventh month of the siege, you had lost another ten thousand.

On a mound of your fallen warriors, you stood alone against a serpentine hellion—a brute of a Kaza'dur, nigh twice your height and five times your weight. By the fading light of glorious dusk, you battered the monstrous fiend as blood and sweat flowed like rivers down your face and your arms. The beast lashed out with one of many hands, clamped down on your shoulder with fanged, venomous fingers, and pulled, tearing away your shield arm.

It mattered not—you thrust your holy longsword through the beast's eyes, slaying it in an instant.

Splayed, bleeding out atop a macabre dune, then washed crimson by the lifeblood weeping from your countless slain followers, a prayer rolled off your lips. Who could blame you for calling upon the Goddess? Certainly, I'd have done the same in your stead.

An angel appeared standing over you, an avatar of Dusk's will, made manifest. Oh, how the goddess loved you, Cain! She swept you up in her arms and took you into the barren skies, her wings a lone ebon cloud. For the first time since the Arrival, the desert was watered. Her sorrow rained upon the desolate sands as the Goddess wept for you.

Dying in her embrace, she asked you a simple question. "My love, will you allow me to save you?"

"My love..." You groaned. Your final thoughts fled to your poor Anastasia, wasting away throughout your prolonged— soon, permanent—absence; then to your daughter, languishing in matters of court without the guidance and advocacy of her father, and to your unborn son, stilled in the womb... a special pain, one you never learned to heal from. Oh, how you wished you'd have done it all differently!

For fear of never seeing your family again, you gave yourself to the Goddess in the sky, over Idraan.

"Renew your vow, dear Arthur," the Goddess said. "Repeat those words I desire so...."

"I... will," you rasped, your life's blood nearly spent. "... never stop... loving." With your last breath, you swore: "I devote myself... body and soul."

Thus, you were forever bound. The Goddess embraced your soul, weaving it with her own, claiming you for eternity. As your souls coalesced, so too did mind and body so intimately intertwine. Your own skin mottled and morphed; you and Dusk descended from the heavens as one.

Reborn, you took on the aspect of Dusk Incarnate. With divine wrath, you assaulted and systematically dismantled the Kaza'duran facilities inside their alien city. With cold, unfeeling hands, you swept your blade in flaming arcs, reaping the souls of any unfortunate enough to live within the walls. Dusk—you—delivered holy revenge upon the snakes of Idraan, and even upon the people they had bound in chains. For the slaves of the Kaza'dur were tainted, infected, and their corruption, their weakness, could not be allowed to spread.

You claimed Idraan for humanity, driving the invaders to near extinction within the dark of a single night, known now as The Night of Tears. You traded your very soul so that some might live, taking everything from others in the process.

How cruel, then, that all of it was for naught.

You returned home to Undton, to your family—but you had changed. Your men carried you, a husk of your former self, a shell harboring power mortals are not designed to contain. How did you persist so long, carrying all that weight? Yes, I see the pain fluttering across your face. Is this the first time you've relived those last few strides of your life, those precious final months, given to you in exchange for your soul—and those of everyone else?

Morgana's pestilence was what brought your keep to ruin. Traders unwittingly carried it from your holdings to Daizeton, and beyond. It spread across the Valentine outlands and ravages the living to this day. Ever evolving, the plague proliferated, and neither borders nor seas could contain it. The Goddess Corrupted had left her mark upon your body, and your frail, mortal frame was not sufficient to quell the chthonic power festering within you.

You had become pestilence; it seeped out your very pores, poisoning the world around you. When finally you died... a mere season after Dusk—Morgana—saved you, your poison bloomed, enveloping countless souls within its black embrace.

Do you remember the night before you died?

Anastasia was in the beginning stages of the illness, ignorant of the destruction awaiting you all come sunrise. Sitting by your side, she was as withered and frail as you had become. She folded your hand in hers, always so soft and tender. Part of you resented her for that—your hands had always been hard and cruel; hers had only nurtured life, while you had only extinguished it.

"My love..." she whispered, unable to look into your sallow eyes. "What are we to do now?"

Your head lolled towards her. Anastasia was naught but an amorphous blur; the pestilence had taken your sight—as it had mine. "How is Kat? I wish... to see her."

"She's gone, Cain. You know that."

"Oh..." You pondered this. Yes, you had known. Anastasia had written you before the siege. "Where has she gone?"

Tears welled in her eyes. "I don't know."

You sighed—no, you groaned, years of your life were expelled with your breath as your body deflated, shrinking before your wife's very eyes. "I only ever wanted the best for you two..."

"And all I've ever wanted was *you*. This is the price I pay for falling in love with a hero."

Your wife was so beautiful. Her skin seemed to glow in the dim, flickering candlelight, her azure eyes sparkling with the gentle sway of the flame. You remembered the waltz you two shared at Vidoq's galla on the night you met, all those years ago.

You smiled. "It's what you get for marrying an orphan with no name... Look at all we have now..."

Anastasia shook her head. "I've always preferred the nameless orphan boy. He'd never leave me to wither in this forsaken castle, grown wretched, all alone for years." She breathed deep, belabored by her failing lungs. "No... only Syr Arthur the Hero did that."

You sat up, suddenly enraged.

"What was I to do?" The only answer to your question was a fit of gurgling coughs, painting your handkerchief red. "I wrote... all I could."

She rose, exhausted by the excuses she had heard time and time again. Those well-intentioned lies you told to ease her pain—and yours. But lies are lies, my dear friend, regardless of your intent.

Anastasia showed you her back, unable to bear looking at you any longer. You watched her pronounced shoulders tense, corded with sinew, and none of the soft padding a Lady of her station ought to have protecting her from famine.

"Cain..." She clenched her fist.

"Stasia?"

"Your heart was never mine, was it?"

Your wife departed before you could protest. Not that you had the breath to do so, coughing the way you were, as your throat closed. You did not wake the following morning... nor did anyone else.

IV

Grahtzildahn, second layer of Pandemonium

Within the frigid depths of the Burning City, Kateryna shivered in a dark and lonely cell. Her stomach growled, roiling in protest to the viscous slop served in a rusty bowl at regular intervals. Even with the meals, she starved. As she grew hungrier, her shivering worsened, further progressing her malnourishment. Accompanying the bitter chills and dizzying fever was the persistent diarrhea—as if her body simply refused to digest the putrid rations.

Muffled conversations slogged through the humid corridors. Guards spoke in unintelligible tongues, their hollow voices emanating from their breast plates, rather than their helms. Kateryna had only caught a glimpse of the metal soldiers patrolling the dungeon.

The crash into the city had been too chaotic… and still her heart burned with grief.

When the metal soldiers had encircled her and Seth, she could not even stand. Collapsed over Montauk, Kateryna wept, her callused hand resting atop the griffin's slowing heart. Though surrounded, the soldiers had not interfered, as if awaiting her out of some twisted sense of honor. Perhaps they reveled silently in their victory, in her pain. It was only after Montauk's heartbeat had ceased that she felt hot, steel hands lay upon her, binding her with hot, iron cuffs.

How long have I been imprisoned here?

Time is meaningless in Pandemonium. Days pass in
seconds, and seconds prolong into hours. There was no way to
know.

Hunger came and went. Diarrhea came and went. Sleep
eluded her mostly, its timid approach oft interrupted by the
hollow clamor and heavy footfalls of roving metal soldiers.
Since waking last from a rare, fitful bout of slumber, Kateryna's
chest ached, the shredded sacks of her lungs filling steadily with
blood and mucus. Head ponderous, thoughts swimming, she
could hardly recall where she was, where she was headed. In
some ways, the hellish prison she found herself in was not so
horrible. At least she was fed, and she enjoyed the feel of solid
ground. For a tormented soul, lesser torments began to seem
like paradise.

Kateryna doubled over, vomiting into the rusty chamber
pot. Her knees buckled at the acrid stench, at the bitter taste
the spew left on her tongue. She fell, curling into a ball on the
frigid stone floor that stole all warmth from her.

Bright vistas of green craggy mountains flashed behind
her eyelids. A dot of light zipped from corner to corner of her
periphery, leading her from one image to the next.

So gorgeous…

She had made it as far as the coastal city of Ionia before
she heard the news. Standing on a glassy beach, caressed by the
gentle push of the wind, under the rustling sway of date palms,
Kateryna heard a crier shouting on the pier, proclaiming that
Don Arthur Cain of Undton had finally defeated the Kaza'dur.
And that he had done so in a single night, razing the sandstone
walls of the Otherworldly City, with only the strength of
his sword arm. More than half of his forces had perished in
the campaign, but humanity stood triumphant before those
serpentine horrors.

Why did I go back?

Whether 'twas some misguided hope she might have a father again, or her shirked obligation to her mother, she was not sure. In the end, it mattered not. Perhaps she was afraid the snakes would retaliate and level her home as her father had theirs—but that was not at all what Kateryna had found upon her return.

Desolation. Ruin. Bodies strewn about the yards. Servants, soldiers, and serfs alike littered the grounds, skin charred with black boils, their bellies bloated with noxious gases— some having already burst in the summer heat. The sight was horrifying. The smell was worse—the acetous malodor of rot and bile, and also that of unremittent sorrow.

She had asked herself then, and she wondered now, *how does one smell sorrow?*

Ignorant that she had been marked by Death for simply entering the keep, Kateryna ventured deeper inside in search of her mother. It did not take long to find her... *Oh gods, how have I forgotten? Was the fog a mercy, after all, Dread Angel? Have you spared us unknowable pain by withholding these memories?*

Within her parents' bedchamber was Mother Death's greatest rendition, a masterwork of suffering, a sculpture of bone and flesh. Cain's body sat upright against the wall, Anastasia suspended in his arms. An armature had blossomed from his neck, vines of pulsing crimson that overtook the chamber, creeping up and along the walls and bursting out the windows, wilding the very seat of civilization.

So grotesque, so undeniably gorgeous—and unfit for mortal eyes.

Kateryna did not remember how long she had lingered there, absorbing the lurid beauty splayed out before her. She could not tear her eyes from the mutilated forms of her parents, but was sure she could feel the serpentine fingers of the vines begin to coil around her ankles, her wrists, her throat...

A memory of forsaken love flashed through her mind, expelling the creeping miasma suffocating her, and Kateryna fled. *And then I found you, my love...*

When she reached the gates of Daizeton, the nightman brought her before Lord Derrida Aslor. The gaunt man could not bring himself to look Kateryna in the eyes, nor did he have the courage to speak. Instead, he made a curt gesture, ordering his chaplain to escort her to the cemetery.

She had fallen to her knees before a newly filled grave.

"Such pain, my dear Kateryna," said a man's voice, somewhere in the dark. "Fret not. I understand you."

"What?" Kateryna sat upright on the floor. "Who's speaking?"

"You are in my care now, child. In my home."

"Grahtz..." she whispered, and shivers marched along the trace of her spine—as if simply uttering his name were enough to progress her festering pestilence.

"Tell me, Kateryna..." The walls reverberated with his exhalations. "Why did Morgana send you here?"

His voice seemed to emanate from below, boiling up from the fathomless depths of the pit itself, though she heard him as if he stood beside her... But Kateryna was alone, freezing beneath the heat of the Burning City.

"Morgana did not send me—I must ascend the Great Stair."

A great guffaw bellowed through the corridors of the cell block, gusting through the wrought iron bars trapping her, knocking her to the ground. The Demon King Grahtz laughed, and the walls buckled and quivered under the weight of his mirth. The floor shook as steam hissed between the cracks in the cold flags. Kateryna's fever pitched, and her world spun. She groped for the satchel Ibrahim had bestowed her, but like the Sun Spear of Dawn, it was gone.

"My dear girl!" cried Lord Grahtz. "Understand, what you ask is impossible. Do you not know why I have erected this city?"

Kateryna clenched her teeth as her head boiled. She gripped her forearms, her nails breaking skin as her stomach rolled, clenching as if a stone was tumbling through her intestines. "You protect the Stair… and thus the mortal world from the damned."

All at once, her symptoms cooled as the temperature dropped from feverish heat to a nauseating chill. The cell sighed, as if in deep contemplation.

"Lord Grahtz, I beseech you. Permit my passage. I am charged by Dawn to carry out this task."

"Oh, my dear girl," cooed the soothing voice of the Demon King. "I am aware of your errand. For you are in my house, and I see the dreams of all who rest their heads on my pillows. I cannot allow you to complete your quest, though I wish I could. Truly, I yearn to grant us both what we desire. But if I allow you to ascend, my city, and the world above, will fall."

"My charge has nothing to do with—"

"Silence!" The ground tilted; what was flat became vertical, and Kateryna slid down the wall-once-floor, landing hard on her shoulder. "Do not dare rebut me, child! In this realm, I am God!"

Searing pain wracked Kateryna's body, loosening her bowels and voiding her stomach all at once. The assault emptied her of everything until only the acidic taste of bile lingered in the back of her throat, chunks of food lodged in her sinuses. Coughing, spitting, she took in a tremulous breath, her eyes hot with tears and ruptured blood vessels.

"Apologize!"

She shook her head, her brains sloshing like seawater in her skull.

"Apologize, child!" The Demon King's roar pulverized whatever shred of will that yet remained to her.

"Forgive me…" Kateryna stammered, the mere act of speaking causing unbearable pain, like needles pressing into her eyes. "Forgive me, my lord."

The room then became perfectly temperate, the air still. All discomfort fled her at once. A torch ignited in the corner of the room, illuminating a simple bed dressed in plain covers. She scrambled to it like a rat abandoning a sinking ship. Kateryna had not even seen a proper bed since before she died.

"I am not a vindictive benefactor…" Grahtz's voice was like a warm fire in the heart of winter. "But I am not to be trifled with. You will come to learn, dear Kateryna, that I am superior to the Dusk and the Dawn—even to that of the High Noon. I am the furnace fueling the summer, the fire that cleanses the waking world of the vermin seeking to escape their just damnation."

"You must know, Lord Grahtz," Kateryna said before taking a ragged breath. "That neither I, nor my people, deserve this fate. We were taken by Morgana's pestilence—a cosmic wrong, never answered for." The words flowed from her mouth with ease, yet Kateryna did not know whence they came. Now that they had been spoken, however, the explanation rang true to her ears. The keep, the blossoms, the rains… "Please, reconsider the status of my soul in your court."

"Yes, child. I know what happened. I know that your soul was not destined for Pandemonium… but since the Dread Angel first sat upon her unholy throne, few who have entered Pandemonium's gates belong." Grahtz paused, his consideration palpable. "Yes, dear Kateryna, I will assist you—with one stipulation."

Do not jump into his arms. A devil always speaks slant.

"I would hear your conditions."

"Allow Morgana's pestilence to take you. Then, join my legion. Join your fellows from Monrovia, so carelessly discarded in her fury by the Dread Angel. Your body will be impenetrable, your will infallible, your strength inexorable! When you wake with a beating heart, you will be reborn in my sight and named anew. Then, and only then, will I permit you to ascend my Great Stair and fulfill your destiny."

Kateryna froze, staring at the wall for minutes, hours, years… How many of her kin had been taken by the Demon King? And was this fate truly the best they could hope for? She breathed deep, the compacted mucus in her lungs vibrating her chest cavity, and she earnestly considered the Demon King's offer.

At last, and only once she was sure of her decision, Kateryna answered: "I cannot accept your terms, my lord, gracious though they are."

The Demon King of Grahtzildahn let out a forlorn sigh, his gentle warmth withdrawing from Kateryna, leaving her to languish in encroaching cold for all eternity. "Then it is here you must remain, child."

In the hellish depths of the Pit of Grahtzildahn, Kateryna Cain of Undton was sentenced to an eternity of isolation, spent in darkness, for her divine charge was too dangerous for the good Demon King to allow her to continue unsupervised.

Kateryna sat in her bed, the one comfort granted to her in countless lifetimes of suffering. She contemplated her many misfortunes, her numerous losses, and her failure to live up to the legacy placed upon her shoulders as the noble daughter of an orphan, turned knight, turned hero. She took in one more ragged breath, inhaling the stench of her disease and her inevitable death and subsequent reincarnation as a lowly, tortured soul.

Yet, despite her grim acceptance of a black fate, she felt a new warmth envelop her against the cold. Not the overbearing pall of the Demon King, nor the disinterested surveillance of the Dread Angel, but a mother's voice, calling her child home. Kateryna closed her eyes and saw the rolling golden fields of her home—not as they were, but as they are.

Kateryna's bare feet embedded themselves in cool dirt. Earthworms emerged from their shallow haunts, wriggling between her toes. Taking in a smooth breath of sweet, living air, Kateryna gazed out at the horizon, where the skeleton frames were being built by the new denizens of Undton. The trees sang their gentle song, and sprouting scallions danced throughout every inch of the fields around her. The morning's warmth poured over her.

Reaching out, Kateryna's hand closed on something solid. Opening her eyes, back in the dank cell beneath Hell and Earth, she again held the Sun Spear of Dawn, its winged tip glowing red hot with the light of the Mourning Sun.

May it light my way, when I need it most....

V

When next I dreamt, I once again inhabited the mind of Invictus, the newly ordained legionnaire of the Reborn Crusade. The Reborn come from all layers of Pandemonium, and many from the Abyss itself, yet something about him rang familiar—Invictus's soul reeked of moldering wood and sickly sea water—and thus he was accessible to me in ways the others of his kind were not, uniquely open to my observations.

Yes, I had met him before. We had both lived in Monrovia and shared an experience that linked us. I settled easily into his perspective, as if he had invited me to wear his plates like my own suit of armor.

I felt Pascal Doon's presence with me, and I wondered if Invictus had somehow invited us both. Unlikely it is, dear reader, that a master wizard and an elder dragon fill one's mind unnoticed.

* * *

I came to know how the dungeons of the good lord's palace had received their namesake. Only once had I been down to the Pit, before I gained my eyes. Even with this otherworldly sight bestowed upon me, I could see little aside from what the faint glow of guttering torchlight revealed: a spiral of cellblocks and corridors embedded within the walls surrounding the Great Stair, which centered the dungeons, plunging from the foundations of the palace and down into the abyss.

In life, I was taught about the eight layers of
Pandemonium—each one uniquely tailored for different
manners of sinners. The priests of my homeland did not know
about the Vale Betwixt, which has retroactively become the first
since the beginning of the Dread Angel's reign. So too, were
they ignorant of the countless folds of Abyss sprawling like so
many festering roots in endless soil.

Hell is only the beginning. Abyss descends farther than even
my wise lord can see. This is why my duty is essential—my duty
is everything.

So many of the lost and damned attempt the climb, to
break free of their eternal judgment. Fools… Treading the
Stair is a perilous venture. The smooth obsidian is slick, and
one could easily slip and fall through the hole bored through
the Earth's crust and into unfathomable depths. Most do not
make it here. But those unfortunate few who do, trade but
one prison for another. For none may walk the Stair and suffer
not the wrath of Lord Grahtz. Yet the good lord is merciful
and recognizes strength. Through his gift, even the lost may be
found and the damned reborn. All they must do is serve…

I had escorted the Dread Angel's riders, a man and a
woman, to their cells as commanded. Once within the cool
interior of the Pit, after leaving the woman to her fate, I took
the man to his own solitary cell, which was to become his
eternal prison. His fear was palpable; I could smell his weakness
like the excrement seething from every tortured orifice of his
plague-wracked body. Surely, I had known him once. We had
both lived beneath the Dread Angel's surveillance, and we both
knew the bitter taste of her disease. Yet, I chose the road to
righteousness, and he, the wicked path to damnation. For that,
I could not forgive him, no matter our shared origin, nor would
I pity him his ill fate.

"You are scum," I said, sealing him away forever. "How dare
you be so arrogant as to think you could invade our great city?"

I assumed the man would utter some vile nonsense, shout
obscenities—it is what I would expect from a delinquent of the
Dread Angel's court—but he said nothing. I did not look at

him, nor could I see his expression even if I had, but I felt his contemplative gaze on me just the same.

His insolent restraint enraged me further.

"Have you nothing to say? Is your soul so depraved that you would accept your fate in silence?"

The bars rang as the prisoner wrapped his dirty fingers around them. "Who are you?"

Such an inane question. An insult. Surely, he was losing his mind.

"I am Invictus, sworn legionnaire of the Reborn Crusade. I am your captor."

"No," the man said at length. "That can't be."

"Silence, swine!"

"Who are you?" the man asked again before he was consumed by a coughing fit. "Before this..." he struggled to breathe. "What was your living name? Grant me this one kindness..."

The man's stubborn insistence disturbed me. It was not his words, but the earnest quality to his tone—the familiarity of his voice. I wondered how I heard that voice echoing in the annals of my past, of another time, another life, nigh lost to memory.

I turned around. My intention was to enter his cell and beat him into silence, to split skin and break bone under the hammer of my fists, to purge his corrupted flesh of the weakness that ailed him and in so doing, with each blow, purge that which remained of my own. But my newly grown heart skipped a beat as I looked into his eyes, and saw my brother's terror as he took in my monstrous form.

* * *

For days we slept, dreaming of Pandemonium.

After the first night in the observation chamber, we returned to my quarters where again I enjoyed the comfort of my own bed. The headmaster ordered pot after pot of scalding chamomile tea and an entire cask of sleeping powder. I conjured for him a fine guest bed befitting a man of his station. In my retirement, my bank accounts were no longer as abundant as they once were, but the expense was well worth the secrets we worked to descry. Besides, there has never been an invoice I failed to forward to the Citadel's bursars for reimbursement.

Between dreams, we convened in my study, analyzing and interpreting all that we had witnessed, notating as much as we dared remember. Oft we all forget our dreams within mere minutes of waking, and this is no less true for oneiromancers. Details are fleeting, and pesky—it takes much fortitude to hang onto them long enough to prepare paper and quill and ensnare them on the page.

The following events were viewed remotely, over the course of several weeks, between mid-April to early-May of the one-hundred-and-thirtieth year after Arrival. I have worked tirelessly to present a narrative composed of my own experiences, compiled with those of Headmaster Pascal Doon.

* * *

Standing on a ridge, I gazed down into the bluffs and saw the smoky silhouette of the Burning City in the distance, centered by what looked like an ebon needle threading the horizon: the Great Stair. We were close, within a day's walk or an hour's flight on Krakow's back. Arthur's injuries were such that they forced us to remain grounded, damned to an exhausting march over the plains of Grahtzildahn.

Luckily, we had evaded all resistance—with a few close calls.

I stared at the black line splitting the landscape and cursed myself for faltering in my convictions. Command was in my grasp, and indefinite pleasure, unknowable ecstasy… but my heart, beating in the dirt somewhere so very far from me, ached more than my loins. And so, I renewed my oath to Dusk and resolved to shepherd her Chosen to his destiny.

And what of my destiny? What of Citha's?

We had left Citha behind as she had requested. Odds were that she had been devoured by the horde encountered in the Screaming Fields. More likely, she now led a horde of her own. I wondered when I might hear tell of a new commander subjugating the other hellish lords, bending them to her will, and destroying the fools who dared to resist.

Arthur finally made it up the ridge, my Krakow slithering behind him. Arthur's face was gaunt, his hair gray and falling out in clumps. Yet the web of veins in his neck and face pulsed with vigor. The Goddess within him had awakened, seeming to take as much as she had given.

In life, I had always written off the tale that Dusk had possessed Cain, capturing the Kaza'duran city in a single night. I wouldn't know. On the Night of Tears, I was indulging in a brothel at a trading post, one hundred leagues away, that I had all too eagerly volunteered to hold while my companions marched on.

Seeing him—seeing *her*—the calamity that followed our unlikely victory in the Sands now made disturbing sense. For the first time, I now knew those tales to be true. For countless years, that truth was obscured from me. I felt safe then, in my ignorance, satisfied with my lowly position of power under Morgana's heel.

No longer.

"I cannot abide this heat another day," I said, staring at the blackened armature of the Burning City. "I've already marched three years across one desert with you, Arthur. Tell me you're well enough to ride."

My friend stood tall, despite the weight he carried. He breathed deep, and even in the full light of day, I felt the blistering waves emanating from him. Ever more, he looked like a corpse, but embodied incomprehensible greatness. *Be he zealous fanatic or unwavering demigod?*

Tightening his fist around the hilt of his sword, he said: "Yes—but we fly not to the gates."

I sighed. "Then how do you presume to enter the blasted city?"

"There is a cave mouth on the outskirts of the city, outside the walls, that leads underground," Krakow spoke into our minds. *"We will enter through the Pit."*

I swung about, gaping at my mount. "How in Hell do you know that?"

"Another form... I had been sentenced to eternity in the Pit. I can only attribute my freedom to chance. A Reborn had gone berserk, driven mad by endless servitude, and beaten me to a bloody pulp. Our once-mistress plucked my soul from the ether, weaved for me this avian body, and bound me to you."

"And why, my most formidable companion, have you withheld this information from me?"

"I've told you this tale, Syr Derrida, many times. You do not listen."

I watched a lizard chase a scurrying field mouse between craggy rocks at our feet. Blackened roots crept through the cracks in the arid soil, withered in the furnace heat of the plains. Say what you will of the administrators of Pandemonium—at least the Demon King maintained order, an ecosystem within his realm. All Morgana had done with her near infinite power— was build a bloody sewer.

"Our children have likely been captured," Arthur said. "I will not allow my daughter this fate. I have forgotten her too many times... I will not do so again."

A waterwheel churned in my guts, transmuting my organs to sludge. But I did not protest. I was so sick of being a coward.

* * *

Armed with the radiance of Dawn, Kateryna sawed at the iron bars enclosing her cell with the incandescent blade of the Sun Spear. The sycamore haft was warm. Just holding it invigorated her atrophied muscles. The Mourning Sun fueled Kateryna, and in turn, her own will fueled the spear. Kateryna shined a glorious solar, the physical embodiment of Great Mother Birth. Unlike her dark mirror, Dawn had bestowed a mighty gift unto her Chosen. Within minutes, Kateryna freed herself from her eternal prison, and by sheer luck, not a soul tarried in the corridor to stop her.

Pulled by unconscious certainty, Kateryna approached the open ledge, her bare toes hovering over bottomless depths. She looked up, beheld the Great Stair in all its foreboding grandeur. A single spiral column, hewn from a shaft of obsidian, was all that stretched between Life and Death, between the waking world and the Abyss.

Further along the corridor, Kateryna heard tortured souls screaming, begging for sweet release that would never come, then the ascending sequential footsteps of the patrolling legionnaires. Guilt poked its ugly head at the back of her mind. In life, she had abandoned Seth just as her father abandoned her—yet Seth had not survived the heartbreak. Now, with the unknown fate of her mother resting on her shoulders, Kateryna was confronted by an impossible decision.

"I'm sorry..." she whispered into the isolating darkness of the descending corridor. "Our happiness was never accounted for."

With the strength of Dawn, the Mourning Goddess, Kateryna lept from the ledge, soaring above the infinite void, landing painfully on her chest against the sharp edge of the Stair. Using the Sun Spear for leverage, she hauled herself onto the slick, obsidian steps.

"I promise," she said between labored breaths. "I will set things right."

* * *

"How in the fuck is it so cold down here?" I groaned, shivering—bloody shivering—within the fiery depths of Grahtzildahn. "How much longer, Krakow?"

"We are drawing near, Syr Derrida."

Arthur's strides were long, and I took two steps for
every one of his. The paradox of his continued existence was
striking. Even in the wan glow of my lantern, I saw sinkholes
darkening his features, the shape of his skull so pronounced I
hardly recognized him. He was a shell, barely withholding the
boundless power of the goddess.

I understood none of it—I just wanted it all over with.

"And what will you do then, my most contemplative master?"

Get out of my head, you bloody bird. We've discussed this.

"There's nowhere to go. We've betrayed the mistress."

In an ideal world, I would have little need for a mistress
going forward. But those were just hopes, and I had no clue
how to maintain my newfound sovereignty in the days to come.
Perhaps I might return, fall to my knees, and beg for mercy.
My plans, such as they were, came and went with every step
I took in those wretched tunnels, dashed and rewritten every
time I remembered the gentle sway of Morgana's divine bosom
beneath her silks.

Arthur cleared his throat; something in his chest rattled
as he took his next breath. He was a walking bag of bones. I
might have been tired, and damned frustrated, but I had already
followed that man to Hell and back—in every sense of the
phrase—and I was not keen on the notion of his demise.

At least… for as long as I could reasonably accompany him.
*I love the man—but I'm not setting foot on that bloody staircase
again.* I shivered at the thought; the horrors I had experienced
on my singular, solitary descent into Sloth.

"We're here," Arthur said, his deathly timbre reverberating
through the stone surrounding us.

"Welcome to the Pit, Syr Derrida."

"Let's keep our stay short, shall we?" I said, fondling the hilt
of my ruined smallsword.

We emerged from the tunnel into a wide chamber, torches lining the walls and running in unending spirals in every direction. Despite the torchlight, we were consumed by viscous black. I had expected a greeting party of armed interlopers, but there was nothing save for the stench of shit and piss, the wretched cries of the damned, the cracking of whips, and the whir of chthonic machinery.

Arthur muttered incomprehensibly under his breath, his voice suddenly feminine—the voice of Dusk. I blinked, and now I saw clearly the desolation of the Pit; the stained floors and jagged walls, the all-too-narrow ledge, and a glorified manhole that must have led to an altogether more unpleasant doom.

Yet, still, there was no patrol to be seen.

"He is expecting our arrival," said Dusk through the withering mouth of my friend. "He feels me—and I feel him."

"Erotic."

Arthur grabbed both my shoulders, his manic, dark eyes trained on mine. In his own voice, he said: "We free our children, then confront Grahtz."

"You've lost your fucking mind!"

"Do you think he will simply allow us to walk out of here? The Demon King must perish if we are to survive."

I shook my head, shrinking from his grasp. "You can't be serious... This is mad!"

"Flee if you want, Derrida," Arthur said, tossing me aside before striding up the corridor. "Either way, I will do what I must. I didn't expect your help, anyhow."

Krakow padded silently behind him, leaving me blustering alone. I watched Arthur's back for a time, considered turning around. Once he stepped from my sight, everything again went black. I cursed under my breath and ran after him.

* * *

For the first time, my new heart ached—the heart I had grown, I had earned. I knew my prisoner spoke true. He was my brother, and he had travelled an immeasurable distance to find me, only to be repaid with unending peril. In every way, I was torn. Loyalties divided, memories fragmented, my body and soul were at war.

"Say your name…" Seth collapsed to his knees, tears streaming down his face. "You must remember!"

"I am Invictus…" I insisted, as if my voice were not ruled by my heart. Something died inside of me as I watched my brother's expression fall. "So too, was I once your brother. I remember now… My name was Isshiah Aslor, of Daizeton. I perished of the Dread Angel's plague soon after you took your own life… Why did you, brother?"

I watched Seth's stubbled jaw quiver; his eyes widened with sorrow. "I did not think—"

"No, you did not. You thought only of yourself, of your own sorrow."

"I left you alone," he said, breathing heavily, "but I have come far, and this time, I will not leave you."

"After I was slain by Morgana's herald," I said, all warmth fleeing from my tempered enclosure, "I was brought here, where I have lived and toiled for nearly thirty years. I am Invictus. Whether you meant for it or no, I have lived on my own, and I have found my calling."

"Thirty years…" My brother's tears ceased, his countenance ambivalent. The catharsis of learning the truth is oft accompanied by the emptiness of the mystery's absence. Moments passed before he spoke again. I have no way of knowing how long we stood in silence. Perhaps a year, perhaps but a minute.

"Isshiah… please. If not me, then free Kateryna. She must ascend the Stair. What's at stake is so much bigger than us! You've lived beneath Morgana's scrutiny, witnessed her folly as I have. Something has been amiss for longer than either of us have existed—but Kateryna can fix it!"

"What is wrong, brother? Tell me that. Then venture to explain how a lone, mortal woman would repair it? You speak nonsense! You've been driven mad by your perilous, foolish journey to save me, Invictus, who never needed saving!"

"I'm... no—"

"You are naive to believe anything that woman told you. Do you not remember the knife she thrust into your very soul?"

Seth nodded meekly. "Of course I do."

"And yet you deign to tell me that she holds some magic key that will right some amorphous, cosmic wrong? You are my brother, Seth Aslor, our souls cannot lie, but the good Lord Grahtz is my liege! He alone has saved me from eternal torment. He alone engineered my superior body! Inside this armor, I have cultivated new innards, a heart wholly my own. How dare you demand I betray these gifts!"

"Stand down, son."

Startled, I swung about, ready to draw my blade. I stayed my hand when my eyes settled on a man I had not seen since my short years in the waking world. My lord father, Syr Derrida Aslor, somehow stood before me. Trailing close behind was another of the Dread Angel's beasts, and her Chosen, the very same who had slashed my throat.

I knelt as any good legionnaire should, a mix of instinct and convoluted rehearsal from the blending of my previous lives. "Father..."

He placed his warm hand upon my shoulder, beckoning me to rise, then swept me up in an embrace. Half my height and horribly thin, it was a strange, disproportionate gesture—yet it had healed a wound that, until then, had been hidden from me.

"Will you free your brother?"

I shook my head. "The good lord—"

"The Demon King will be dead before I leave this place," said Morgana's herald, the master of the raven that had assaulted the palace. His face was gaunt, his skin without color, as if he were becoming dust before my eyes. "Aid us or die—with him."

"Go along with their plan, my Reborn," whispered the good lord inside my mind. *"This confrontation is unavoidable. I would have you by my side when it comes to pass."*

Slowly, I rose and willed Seth's cell open. Together, in silent solidarity, I led that motley crew to the block where Kateryna Cain was held. I knew the good lord had plans for her, and as we came upon the melted bars of her empty cell, it seemed my liege had been hard at work.

My brother fell to his knees. My father placed a reverent hand upon his shoulder. "Can't say I'm surprised, given how she did'ya last time."

"It's not that." Seth wiped his nose with his forearm, black with grime. "I never thought we would escape this place. I'm a sorry fool for thinking she'd need my help."

"Come," the Chosen said, striding up the corridor. "Time is short. We must forge a distraction, so her ascent may go unnoticed."

With that, we ran through the twisting corridors and cell blocks of the Pit. A pit of my own had opened in my heart, as my companions were unshakeable in their resolve to murder the good lord—and already I knew which side I would choose when swords were drawn. In every way possible, I was torn.

* * *

For the second time, the Goddess's power destroyed Cain from the inside out. Though his chthonic form could better withstand the currents of divine energy pulsing through his veins, time was short. With not a moment to waste, Cain strode ahead of his companions, leading them through the empty halls of the Demon King's palace.

Dusk had warned Cain what lay ahead—the Demon King had withdrawn his entire legion so he could flaunt his power for all to witness. Cain knew Grahtz meant to put an end to Dusk, for his own survival depended on the Goddess's final fall.

Thus, the Demon King had to die. There was no alternative. Cain had to descend the Stair. He had to help Kateryna... had to help Stasia. To succeed in his divine mission, every piece must be in place; else the entire foundation whereupon fate rests would crumble. Else, his lifetime of wrongs would go unanswered, unrepented.

Thus the Demon King must perish—this was Cain's conviction.

"This is it, eh?" Derrida said as they passed into the entry hall of the ground floor and came upon the massive double doors, forged of solid brass. "I don't think we get in unless he wants us to..."

"He's expecting us." Cain pointed to the Reborn, once Derrida's younger son. "Open it. Now."

Invictus hesitated but did as he was bid. Pressing his gauntleted hands, filled with mottled flesh and chemically formed bones, against the door, Invictus pushed. They swung open with a resounding clamor.

Cain looked back over his shoulder, his eyes sharp as cold steel. "The Reborn does not serve you. He was your boy, once. But Grahtz's hold on his creations outweighs bonds of blood."

"Aye..." Derrida watched as Invictus crossed the threshold, his lips pale, drawn tight. "Thanks for the tip. What do we do now?"

"Succeed."

Derrida swallowed. "Simple enough."

As the party entered the throne room, an entire legion of Reborn shifted to stand at attention, their stiff movements ringing out like a gong on a mountaintop. All fell silent as Cain led his reluctant procession into battle against a godlike entity in his own demesne.

"The Dread Angel returns to my court at last!" cried the Demon King atop his throne, from which he could not rise. He raised his flabby arms, festering folds hanging from a malformed and malnourished skeleton. "If only I had more time to prepare, I would have—"

The Demon King ceased his vile litany, for he found a flaming longsword had pierced his flaccid throat. "Argh—no..." he gurgled in protest, but the deed was done. In an instant, faster than anyone could perceive, Cain had taken the form of Dusk and, with the blinding speed of a scorned warrior goddess, ended the eons-long reign of Lord Grahtz, Demon King of Grahtzildahn, with a single thrust.

Grahtz groaned and faded from reality; his soul dispersed into the ether, to be gathered and made anew. So too did Dusk fade, towering over the masterless legion, shrinking back to inhabit Cain's degenerating body, as he strode back out the doors whence he came. His errand—and truly, that was all Grahtz was to him—was finished.

Yet so much more remained to be done.

* * *

I fell to my knees, my will snuffed out in an instant. My fellow Reborn stared listlessly at the Herald—without the direction of our liege, we were powerless to avenge his memory. My father was the one to intercept Morgana's Chosen, the assassin of kings.

"I can go no further, Arthur!"

The Chosen stopped. Without looking back, he said: "You've come far enough, my friend. Claim your spoils."

I watched an idea blossom in my father's eyes, a smirk spreading across his narrow face. He flicked his head towards the now-empty throne. His foul griffin, wearing the aspect of the bald eagle native to my homeland, surged with a flurry of wings to envelop Lord Grahtz's seat. Then, Lord Derrida Aslor ascended, sitting upon the throne of Grahtzildahn.

In an instant, my will had been dashed to smithereens. In another, I was restored—torn no longer.

* * *

Pascal Doon and I snapped awake the moment Syr Derrida
sat upon Grahtz's throne. We exchanged glances, unsure if what
we had witnessed was indeed true. A resounding pulse shook
the walls, bringing down paintings and framed maps tumbling
to the floor. Phrygia remained in the clouds for the eleven
days of the academic week, where we were safe from seismic
phenomena—and though an earthquake could never reach us,
the city shook, buffeted by rippling forces shaking reality itself.

"This is unprecedented," said Pascal Doon the Lavender.

"Quite."

"We must intervene. This cannot continue without our
intercession."

"The balance must be restored," I declared, flinging open
the glass door to my balcony, exposed to naught but open sky,
"lest all our souls be damned."

My dear friend followed me outside. We stood together for
a time, him staring out to the horizon, which was no doubt
beyond beautiful in the late afternoon, and I, taking my last
whiff of fresh, salty air, listening to the distant waves of the
Black Sea below.

"You've not yet visited Pandemonium, have you,
headmaster?"

Pascal Doon snorted. "You know I haven't."

"We'll be sure to catch the sights on the way home."

With that, I let the air take hold of me as I leapt from
my balcony. Embraced by billowing winds, I cursed under
my breath as I realized I had again, in my haste, forgotten to
dress. Not a second more had passed before I heard the great
swooping of dragon's wings and felt hard scales embedding
themselves into my bare ass. Pascal Doon the Lavender, one of
the seven living elder dragons, let out a mighty roar. Chanting,
I conjured a new set of travelling robes and opened before us
a dimensional rift leading to Dysmorphia—the ninth layer of
Pandemonium.

FIVE

Today, I have found my god.
She had strayed from me once,
"Follow me!" she commanded,
Then left me bleeding
On cold, slick tiles.

I had asked my family,
All that they knew.
"Love," one said.
"Accountability," nodded another.

Grace in all things, forgiveness in others.
Who is this god we seek?
And why
Hasn't she been revealed to me?

I asked my lord of his god.
And he said, "I have none."
For in his realm,
There is only blood.

I've lived long and hungry,
Awaiting the day,
I'd again know peace.

Today, I have found my god.
She had strayed from me once,
But this day,
Her grace reigns supreme.

Baptiste Fournier (b. -556, death unknown).
"Not Alone," published Year 150, under a pseudonym.

I

Descending the Great Stair

Dysmorphia, ninth layer of Pandemonium

For the second time in my prolonged existence, I descended the steps hewn into the perfect pillar of obsidian driving through our world like a dagger thrust into the earth's heart. I cannot say for how long I walked, for how long I felt the dull impact of every step eroding the bones of my knees and my ankles. But none of that mattered—this journey was my final trial, and the dissolution of all that I had become, my penance.

I owed the world, no, all of creation, an insurmountable debt for my complacency beneath Morgana's command, for the countless atrocities I committed behind the mask of coercion and servitude. Though my mind had been a blank slate, wiped clean each morning before I set out upon my black errands, it was always my blade ending lives—wielded by my hand. My own eyes were the last things my victims saw before their souls departed to whatever black fate awaited them.

I did these things without question, without remorse.

As I descended the Stair, my guilt came upon me all at once, compounding tenfold.

I have never possessed agency over my own life, nor my afterlife. I have long been a pawn in the bloody games of gods and men. Once, I was but an orphan, a refugee, fleeing the war that shook the world. I was happy to serve any cause that saw me fed. I was satisfied to simply do as I was bid. Much of that changed when I met Anastasia, when I first gazed into those wide eyes encompassing the morning sky and countless leagues of windswept tundra. For a moment—just a moment—there was no duty great enough to take me from her. For one fleeting moment, I was hers. And she was mine.

Despite the love I held, so very dear and close to my heart, it was not enough to withstand the malice of the Goddess Corrupted. Morgana—not Dusk, they are different halves sired from a fractured whole—stole my love from me, and sentenced me to mindless servitude. I was torn between my life and my faith, mourning the loss of my worship, my will to choose. To reject the Goddess would have meant my soul's end, or worse, my soul's eternal torment; and so I bowed before her and served.

I am a coward.

With every agonizing step, my knees trembled, and tremors wracked my legs. I shed the weight of my armor, piece by piece, as my strength failed me. I carried the dwindling flame of Dusk in my vacuous chest, devoid of a heart. Despite the echo of her love I felt, despite our shared conviction to cleanse the world of the Dread Angel's corruption, her divine spirit slowly destroyed me from within. This is the nature of such things.

A weight heavier still, a burden bound to my soul, was the shame I felt for my myriad failures, the contempt my family rightly claimed, and the rancorous self-loathing that enshrouded my head in a suffocating miasma. Covered in the blood of so many lives wasted, I withered away with every step I took toward redemption.

"I will never stop…" I whispered, my lungs shriveling with every word.

My oath.

"I will… never stop…"

My conviction.

"I will never stop loving."

My *faith*.

When Dusk first spoke to me, I was a boy floating naked in a hot spring beneath the wartorn savannah of my home. The Goddess, in that moment, had meant those words as they should be taken—she bid I swear to find love, and to cherish it, to protect it, even if it cost me everything. Just as my blood father had done, charging to his death, all those years ago. When corruption took hold of Dusk, and Dusk morphed into Morgana, so too did the meaning of my oath liquefy into mud between my fingers.

As my bare feet touched the black, acidic soil of Dysmorphia, the stinging breeze cut through my exposed flesh and my manhood. I had become a walking tomb. The skin of my hands had decayed, clinging to my bones like a moldering cloth. I had stopped breathing, and had I possessed my heart, surely I would have collapsed at the base of the Stair, at the lowest depth I had ever tread. Surely, I would have fallen into the Abyss, to fall forever, my remains drifting in the endless void roiling beneath Dysmorphia.

I lingered there for a moment, lost in thought.

Shaking away my doubts, I took my first step, guided by Dusk. In the eddy of doubt whirling behind my eyes, I heard a faint echo of her voice as it once was, her dwindling spark guiding my dying body to where I had buried my beating heart.

This had been Morgana's first command. We riders chose a burial ground, known only to us, for there, in the court of the Dread Angel, there is room for her alone. "I will never stop..." The words ripped my esophagus, a sandstorm abrading my vocal cords. But that was but a trifle—my body was my own for the first time. "Never stop..."

Soon, I came upon the barren grove where I had lain myself to rest. Throughout the entirety of Pandemonium, there exists a pulse like heartbeat rippling through the dense earth. I believe it is the beating of hearts lost and stolen, buried and hidden for some eldritch purpose.

If you have lost your heart, you are nothing; and I know
this to be true, for as I knelt into the black soil, the bones of
my legs splintering beneath my paltry weight. I dug with my
fingers, the putrified flesh peeling from my hands. So too did
I feel the rest of myself falling away. Bitter siroccos picked me
apart piece by piece—condors feasting upon the dying doe.

Thump-thump. Thump-thump.

I lifted a rondure from the earth, writhing in my hands.

Thump, thump. Thump, thump.

Beads of damp soil fell from moist flesh.

Thump, thump. Thump, thump.

I pulled a worm from the central vessel, then slotted my
heart into the exposed hole in my chest.

Thump, thump. Thump, thump.

"I will never stop loving..." I swore to the spark still
attached to me, and I fell forward, overtaken by darkness.

Thump, thump. Thump...

* * *

When the spurious radiance of the underworld shone upon
me for the first time, someone pulled me from the earth by my
arms, as another dug away at the clinging soil. The earth birthed
me, and this was my first memory: An old man knelt in front of
me, his complexion sallow and pale, his sunken eyes glazed with
cataracts. A gentle breeze tickled my face, bristled my eyelashes,
tussled my hair.

For the first time, I breathed deep, filling my lungs.
All at once, I was beset with emotions so far beyond my
comprehension.

So I wept.

The old man held me in his arms, with a compassion I had
never known. The thought confused me. How could I put a

word to a sensation I had never known? Surely, I had known some semblance of it… in another life. That thought yet caused more tears to fall.

The old man's companion lingered further down the blackened ridge. He was tall, covered with amethysts, and possessed the horned head of a beast, resembling the Elder Dragons of old—and he was distressed. I could feel the tension radiating from him as much as I could feel the heat burgeoning within the swollen glands inside his throat.

"By the gods, above and below…" my savior cooed in my ear, his warm breath tickling the hairs on my neck, "you've made it. I can't believe you've made it."

I did not understand; I could only weep, ululating with ecstasy and uncanny remorse. Something within me wanted to scream, "I'm alive! I'm alive!" over and over, bawling in a strange man's arms, who held me as a father should. At first, I thought he was my father.

The old man gazed into my eyes with his milky, sightless portals. "My friend, I will tell you everything there is to know."

He told me the tales of my life, my death, my afterlife, and rebirth. As he wove his words, images and scenes flashed before my mind's eye, supporting the truth of what he claimed. By the end, my eyes had gone dry, arid like the desert that had claimed countless souls beneath my charge.

No longer an infant, I was again that hard man who had failed so many times.

"But you will not fail this time," vowed my savior. "You have come too far—and so have we." He gestured to the dragon-man who had yet to introduce himself.

"There is one final errand," I said, remembering Ibrahim's prophesying chorus in his hut lodged within the threshold between Morgana and Grahtz—now, Lord Derrida. "I must retrieve the sword forged from the blood of a thousand heretics… and thrust its point into the heart of evil."

"Yes…" The old man stroked his scraggly beard, which was so long the frayed edges of it tickled my exposed thighs. "I've been pondering that for some time."

"Several leagues to the north," said the dragon-man, his voice shockingly eloquent coming from such a savage maw, "there stands the Temple of Abandon. Within, you will find the custodian of the underworld—the Watcher of the Abyss. The Watcher will be your guide."

The old man leapt to his feet and balled his fists. "How would you know?"

"I chanced upon a passage in my reading the morning we departed. 'The Abyss Watcher knows no god nor faith, for it must stand vigil before the darkness in stalwart defiance of the encroaching Abyss.'"

"Astrofus! Argh, how dare you utter his purloined prose in my presence."

"Like it or no," the dragon-man tittered, "the man knew the cosmos well." He turned, pointing to a gray rooftop peaking above the hills in the distance. "If your role in all this is truly prophesied, Lord Cain, then it is no coincidence that you buried your heart in the very demesne where lies your charge."

"If the Watcher does not possess the weapon you seek," said the blind man, "then it will know who does. Go now, my friend, and march into the darkness with renewed vigor. Set right the myriad wrongs. Restore the balance… for all our sakes."

"Who are you? How do you know all this?" I shook my head, thoughts amuck. "We've never met—I'm sure of it—yet you both are so familiar."

"Dreams, my friend, are powerful things."

The dragon-man sighed. "I am Pascal Doon, Headmaster of the Citadel and Governor of Phrygia. I remember the day you were knighted and legitimized in the Valentine court, Lord Cain. We celebrated your ascension as a beacon of progress. In the days of the Old Empire, only the aristocracy were allowed to rise."

I nodded, unsure what to say. Introductions felt like a petty waste of time beside the mountains standing before me.

"And I, my friend," said the blind man, "have been dreaming of you for years. I wept the day I learned of your family's cruel demise. It then became my obsession to find out what happened to you. I've witnessed much of your service to the Dread Angel, and I've lived in Monrovia in the flesh. I worked the docks with your daughter, raising the pilings against the unceasing rise of the sea."

"You call yourself Fulcrum, don't you?" He had never taken one of the stale loaves I raffled off to the starving Monrovians, even when his lot was drawn.

"An alias, as all wizards keep. To know one's given name is to own them. My chosen name, with which I credit my numerous writings, is Phrygian Black. Pascal Doon and I raised the Citadel, and we tend to it still."

My eyes widened, and again I was nearly overtaken with tears. These were great men before me, greater than I in every sense. I was not worthy of their respect nor their aid. I was not worthy, yet I had been given a chance. Shaking both their hands, I bid them farewell and swore to myself I would not squander it.

"We will await your triumphant return," Phrygian Black said. "Once you recover the fabled blade and make your final ascent up the Stair, we shall stand with you against the Dread Angel."

Thus, I strode with determination, with an alien sense of weightlessness in every step. Equipped with only my battered longsword and a spark in my heart, wearing nothing, not even a loincloth to hide my shame from the denizens of Hell, I made for the Temple of Abandon to seek audience with the Abyss Watcher, custodian of the underworld, where finally I would reclaim my honor.

II

Kateryna's eyes ached as she emerged from the darkness. The tender rays of the Mourning Sun shone on her fair skin, mild compared to the furnace heat of Grahtzildahn. Taking her first step from hard obsidian into wet sand, she wiggled her toes and stared out at the lapping waves of the shore. The water was viscous, silver—appearing as quicksilver.

Exhausted, Kateryna collapsed into the sand, holding her knees to her chest. Her journey had been uneventful, save for the countless hours of sightless ascent once the Stair incised the ceiling of the underworld, travelling leagues up through the earth's crust.

Now, that was all behind her—beneath her. Morgana's plague seemed to fade away, as if her unearthly powers bore no authority in the waking world, where her holy sister reigns supreme. For the first time, Kateryna breathed deep and tasted only sweet autumn air.

All around, birds chirped and insects droned. She recognized the vibrating shrill of a red-winged blackbird, the descending staccato of a northern cardinal, native to the boreal forests of the Wyse and the northern tip of Lake Valentine.

She dared not move for fear it was all an elaborate ruse, a cruel illusion woven by the Demon King meant to torment her, to drive her mad. But the scene before her did not dissipate as she observed the sway of every blade of emerald grass. A soothing breeze kissed her neck, carrying the sweetness of honeysuckle and jasmine.

It's spring.

She repeated the words in her mind.

Such majesty…

Eventually, and only when she was ready, Kateryna rose and took a trepidatious step along the animal trail following the stream. Everything remained where it was. Material. Intact. This was neither fading dream nor cruel delusion.

This is real. This is life abounding.

Kateryna wandered, following the pull of the river. The terrain soon became rocky, covered in overgrown brambles that painfully scored her bare feet, blackened with the soil of Pandemonium—now falling away in favor of the red earth of the clay-rich riverbank.

The Sun Spear of Dawn had quelled its sorcerous emanations, the tip cooling and returning to ordinary, pock-marked iron. There was no need to shine any longer… not in the presence of the true celestial body suspended in time and space. She used the spear as a walking stick to traverse the jagged outcroppings. For that purpose, it served just as well as it had as a weapon.

The wind blew, carrying with it a voice calling her farther downstream. It bade she take her time. She did. She moseyed along, her eyes to the sky. *What is this sensation?* Could it be peace?—No, something greater, more profound. The word came to her mind unbidden: *stillness.*

Be still, she thought to herself, though the words were not her own. *Be still, for the days are long and meant to be savored.* Kateryna sat on a rock, stared across at the opposing bank.

Deciduous trees stood sentinel, casting shade over the paths trodden by white-tailed deer and black bears, hanging avenues travelled by squirrels and martens.

Be still...

When she was a girl, the shadows within the thick canopies of the Valentine Kingswood were frightening, conjuring fear of grumpkins, beguiling scoundrels waiting to swallow you whole. Now, she saw the interlapping boughs for what they were: administrators of a complex web of life.

Kateryna had come to know darkness in truth. The forest was nothing to fear, for it was governed by nature—not by minds.

She bore witness to her father's regicide, watched him morph, borrowing the guise of the Valkyrie to slay the Demon King with a single stroke. Then she ran, slicing her feet to ribbons on the sharp edges of the steps until her soles burned, slick with blood.

Despite everything, her father had paved the way for her. Just as she witnessed his countless atrocities, so too had she seen the fog flee his eyes, leaving behind a man she had never met. A man finally free of a lives-long captivity.

"I forgive you."

Kateryna knew she would never have the chance to say it to his face, though part of her held hope that he had heard, wherever Fate had taken him. His actions since awakening from the Dread Angel's fugue had forced her to reconcile with her own failings—and just like her father before her, her foibles were countless.

Unforgivable.

"Be at peace, father..."

Reprehensible.

"Forgive me, too..."

For many were those words intended. She remembered the beautiful night beneath the plains of Grahtzildahn. The temperate waters, an impossible miracle.

"Forgive me."

Kateryna could see Seth in her mind's eye. He was beaten and torn, frail, starving. Yet he wore a smile. Perhaps all was healed in the end. Perhaps.

Something fell into her tangled hair. She brushed it free, sending a gnarled ball of burrs to roll into the water and float away. She looked up, found thick boughs hovering above her, branches forking so sunlight passed through them like a spotlight, leading her eye over her shoulder. Behind her, surrounded by long grass and chromatic wildflowers, stood the largest sycamore she had ever seen.

Kateryna collapsed before the tree's splendor, entirely overcome. All at once, the grief she had been holding back for so long, clouded by ceaseless toil and mind-numbing smog, flooded over her and swallowed her in a blanket of regret and loss...

So much loss.

Writhing in the soil, Kateryna wailed, abandoning the old life, and screamed her nascent release from the womb of perdition.

And then, it was over. The tears ran dry, and all that remained was a woman who had seen the lowest depths of existence and survived to bathe in the sun. That simple truth, that the worst had passed, accompanied peace unimagined. She rose to her knees and hugged the trunk of the sycamore, her entire arm span naught but a fraction of the tree's massive circumference. Ear to the bark, she heard a gentle pulse like heartbeat... and felt the warmth of her mother's soul.

I found you.

* * *

Somewhere in the Wilderlands

West of Kuzolova, South of the North Sea

On the bank of the River Acheron, whose silver streams soon faded to pure azure, Kateryna lived off the land under the watchful protection of her mother's soul tree. She spent the days listening to the wind and watching the birds, learning what the Wilderlands offered—and she found the land was generous.

With dead fallen limbs, she built a shelter, padding it with evergreen branches to shield against the wind. She subsisted on blueberries and soft bark. Some days harkened back to her majestic homecoming; others bemoaned rain and bitter memories, relived in restless dreams. Most days, thankfully, came and went without circumstance.

As weeks stretched into months, and months dissolved through the years, Kateryna's garden grew and prospered. Once she required the comfort of a *home* beyond that of simple *shelter,* she crafted her tools and set to building that home. On the day she finished clearing ground to lay the foundation, a man carrying a pickaxe wandered into her sacred demesne. At first, she did not recognize him, but one look into his deep, brown eyes—now bordered by wrinkles and dark circles— revealed the man for who he was.

Kateryna confronted her love, supported by the ever- watchful gaze of her mother's soul tree. Looking her in the eyes and saying not a word, Seth only smiled, showing her all his crooked, yellow teeth. She collapsed into his arms, and they sank together into the soil and wept their sweet refrain.

Together, they built their home.

Kateryna borrowed lumber from her forest. Seth freed stone from its tomb. Their home, like all homes, was a mess of incongruity and roundabout logic. Above all, it was a life- long work-in-progress. Keeping up with the grounds and living in harmony with the land they had once taken for granted presented a host of errands they were happy to endure.

In the light of the High Noon, on the anniversary of Kateryna's twentieth year since arriving home—Seth's tenth—Kateryna finally took his hands in hers and swore a vow heard only by the birds and the squirrels and the martens, the Dusk and the Dawn and High Noon, and most of all, their three young, ginger-headed girls.

Communities arose near their homestead. People oft visited the family, bringing goods in exchange for livestock and crops and herbal remedies for common ailments. Talk among the farmers told that the old woman and her daughters could see the dead and bring peace to the living. Thus, more people arrived from near and far seeking comfort and repose against the harsh realities of life. Tales trickled to faraway lands of a seer and her silent husband who had ascended the obsidian steps out of hell to return to life in the waking world.

Legends tell of the stair, but no one has found such a structure, even after myriad expeditions had launched upstream, foolishly seeking the gates of Pandemonium.

The family became known as the Shepherds, named after their flock of multicolored sheep. Their daughters grew up and left to see the wider world. Some went on to sire children of their own.

Seth passed away after his fortieth homecoming, his smile set deep into his thin face.

Kateryna Shepherd, a woman many believed had appeared from dust, tended her flock and her garden, teaching children the ways of the forest and the quandaries of the mortal soul. The night she passed into the Great Beyond, the day after her one-hundred-and-eleventh homecoming, an entire village mourned and celebrated her life. When the headman and his hands entered the empty house built beneath the massive sycamore to retrieve her body, they found no body.

Everything else was clean, organized, and just as it should be. A queer, but ultimately innocuous, detail was the rusty spear hanging above the lintel of the front door. The rotting haft fueled Old Kat's symbolic funeral pyre in the square, but a young widow perched the pock-marked spear tip atop the grave marker at the foot of the Great Mother's Sycamore—a silent testament to a story no one would ever be told.

III

From the collected journals of a mad wizard

And now, my dear, loyal reader, we return to where my chronicle began.

Mounted atop the back of Pascal Doon the Lavender, I surged through the squalor of Dysmorphia—a roiling mass of sparkling amethyst and shining splendor soaring high above the malformed victims skittering in the blackened fields below.

As you well know, there is but one way up and one way down. I leaned onto the dragon's back, and Pascal Doon threaded the needle of time and space, darting through the hollow center of the Great Stair.

In mere moments, we thundered our way through Sloth and Dipherticuli—twisted landscapes warped by the desires of sinners, broiling in their eternal damnation. At least, 'twas how the universe worked before the Dread Angel sat upon the Scarlet Chair.

In the days of yore, Dusk was the benevolent adjudicator of Life and Death, shepherding the beloved, and the accursed, dead to their rightful homes in the afterlife.

Once, souls crossed Her bridge spanning the River Acheron and found peace in the Great Beyond. Once, only the wicked and complacent were thrust through Pandemonium's black gates. Yet, since the Dread Angel's corruption on the seat of her insatiable throne, she hoards every soul within her turgid demesne, feasting upon their souls' blood and starving the Hellish Lords of their fair share.

As we exploded through the throne room of Grahtzildahn, I bemusedly imagined setting eyes upon a startled Derrida and his inherited legion, reluctantly scrambling to defend their new lord. Though I could not bear witness to the incredulous expressions flitting by, I offered a wave and sly wink—a likely unnoticed gesture of good fortune to a man I had come to know inside and out.

Continuing through the narrow aperture in the domed, hammered-brass roof, we emerged into the open, piquant air of the Burning City.

I whispered the coordinates of Monrovia into the dragon's mind. Pascal Doon rotated gracefully and launched like a shooting star in the direction I had given. Approaching the spectral wall warding the encroaching wastes of Morgana, Pascal Doon roared, unleashing a stream of pure ionic sorcery from his great maw, opening a temporary fissure that we traversed harmlessly before the wall healed behind us.

I took in the familiar scent of decadent, moldering hope. I reveled in it. To me, it felt like a long-overdue homecoming. I could hear the desperate screams of lost souls in the distance, the moaning of those eaten alive by the wandering demons inhabiting the forsaken islands and the Screaming Fields.

The elder dragon spoke in my mind: "Your village lies beneath the waves, my friend."

I cannot explain why this summoned a tear to my eye. I accepted his news in silence, black memories of unceasing toil lapping on the shores of my pathos. For most, discovering the ruins of their pestilence-ridden prison might provide a sense of closure. Though logic told me so, I had difficulty accepting that the sinking of the wretched town had indeed been a mercy.

"It is no matter..." I said, wiping my eye clean, flinging my handkerchief into the waves. "The Goddess dwells in a keep to the north."

"I will bring you to the water's edge," said Pascal Doon. "Then, I must retreat to the waking world to rest. You know how to call me, should you require my assistance again."

"Thank you, friend..." I gasped. "Know that I will only call if it's absolutely necessary."

"Don't make promises, Phrygian. We both know how those have turned out for you."

I looked into the distance, my visuospatial perception naught but blurred, brief jolts of light. My imagination painted a lush landscape—a valley devoid of festering waters—restored to the glory the Vale once boasted. I saw evergreens standing stolid vigil, saw squirrels and martens chasing one another through gnarled boughs—I even heard the sweet calls of cardinals, blackbirds, and mother robins; the sounds of spring in a land long deceased.

Have you wondered *why* Morgana's demesne lies horizontally, adjacent to that of Grahtz?

Each layer of the underworld is stacked atop the last like a twisted ladder—or a brutal stairwell—yet the Vale Betwixt was crafted with subversive intention, which had since been butchered by the Dread Angel's ambitions... And it was the Scarlet Chair that forged the Dread Angel from the nigh indestructible ore of Dusk.

"I swear to you," I cried atop the dragon, to no one in particular, "I will see these crimes answered for! Even if it claims my very soul!"

"The cycle is broken," my friend said.

"No one helms the ferry," I agreed. "Yet all will be reforged."

Pascal Doon landed, and I alighted by the water's edge, just a few leagues' hike from Morgana's Great Hall. Shifting back to his bipedal form, we embraced. I knew he lamented sending me alone, but even an elder dragon and grandmaster sorcerer must seek repose after opening a portal to the depths of hell before flying all the way back to the waking world. My reserves were thus still untapped, my potential brimming with anticipation as my sorcery begged me to unleash its fury upon the defilers of reality. We bid each other farewell, and my friend faded from sight, embarking on the long trek home, where I prayed I might soon join him for another few centuries of quiet contemplation.

Steeling myself for the final dregs of my journey, I recalled my walking stick and donned my hood, taking the first step of the most grueling walk of my ancient life. I will spare you the details, for nothing material befell me during my wistful sojourn—nothing aside from the pastiche woven by a lifetime of regrets.

Before long, I stood at the precipice of a great bridge, spanning a ravine that fell into the edge of the Screaming Fields. Towering on the near horizon were the looming ebon doors of Morgana's Great Hall, where she, in her infinite glory, surveilled over the damned, whether they had earned their internment or no.

I felt a heartbeat resounding through the land, pulsing in the soil.

It was I, dear reader, who entered those wretched halls as a herald of what was to pass. It was I, dear reader, who told the goddess of her impending downfall—praying all the while for her resurrection.

IV

Within the mutating landscape of Dysmorphia, paths expand and contract, twist and straighten, at will. Like the serpentine gantlet of intestines filling my restored body, the road was long and fraught with peril. And though the Temple appeared to rise but a short journey ahead, in truth, it stood much farther than linear sight implied.

The execrable demons that wandered Dysmorphia's blackened fields accosted me at every turn. I did not fear them; I possessed a beating heart that fueled my spark. When a flabby, pink gremlin was foolish enough to step in my path, I drew my blade and smote it down with ease. But drones are naught but fodder. More troublesome was the pit fiend tailing me, skulking in the shadows, weaving infernal sorcery to traverse the land as dust. I had nigh reached the temple by the time I wizened to its presence, after the behemoth materialized and barreled into me with six arms and the combined strength of a herd of oxen. The ground stolen from my feet, I soared down a ravine before crashing painfully into a rocky crag.

Undaunted, I rose and drew my blade. A cloud of dust twisted into a cyclone, and the pit fiend materialized once again, now standing three times my height. The earth quaked as it rumbled its deep, guttural laughter. Where most demons were wretched, incongruous things, this one boasted proportional girth and bulk—in other words, it was fit to offer me somewhat of a challenge—enough to put myself to the test.

"I have heard of you, Cain—hugh, hugh, hugh!" Its stomach convulsed as its chortles fumed like steam from twisted mouths dotting its shoulders and flabby pectorals. "And now—hugh, hugh—I will feast upon your precious soul."

I shook my head. There was no time for such trifles. "Stand aside, demon. This warning is the only kindness I offer you."

"You? Warning me?" the demon cried incredulously. "Do you know who I am?"

I turned from the foul beast, disinterested in its maddened tirade.

"I am the Earl of Sundicar—hugh, hugh, hugh—third inheritor of Gluttony! I have travelled too far to be ignored!"

I felt its many heavy hands thud to the ground. I rolled, narrowly avoiding the beast's reckless charge. Pit fiends are arrogance made manifest, and thus the Earl of Sundicar did not expect my anticipating its clumsy ambush. It thundered by like a carriage pulled by a dozen sprinting horses and collided with the hard wall of the crevasse.

Dazed by the collision, the beast recoiled—I lunged, burying my notched blade to the crossguard in its back, piercing both of its hearts. My old sword snapped at the hilt as I tried to pull it free, and the blade melted away with the screaming—dying—hellish lord as its physical form dissolved into a bubbling slop.

Unclothed and unarmed I was, yet after such a display, none dared interrupt my errand again. Drones and soldiers alike shriveled in the radiance of the light emanating from my chest. I was a lighthouse standing vigil in the night, battered by waves that dwarfed my stature, but the old man tending the signal fire performed his duty with unrelenting resilience. So too was I a man scorned by his own actions, his own impotence.

I would not accept failure again—not this time.

* * *

The Temple of Abandon

Dysmorphia, ninth layer of Pandemonium

The Temple of Abandon stood tall. Taller, even, than the great cathedral wherein I was knighted and my life was thrown to the wolves. Built of gray stones of compacted ash, the only semblance of color in the entirety of Dysmorphia lay within the brilliant stained-glass windows. In sweeping arcs of orange, yellow, red, blue, and indigo, they depicted myth beyond my comprehension. Prismatic angels stood in formation, watching over their new world. Each image shone peace, harmony, as if murder and destruction and tyranny were unnatural things birthed by humanity, rather than thrust upon us.

As I pushed open the heavy doors, I was overcome by the aroma of frankincense and lavender. I crossed the threshold and was swallowed by shadows, subsumed by void. I called out, answered only by the echo of my own voice. For as long as I could stand, I waited. For years, or for hours, I cannot know. As I lingered, I questioned everything I had accomplished until this point. When I could wait no longer, I turned around to find the door had vanished, replaced by a hunch-backed Skanu wearing a bloody rag wrapped around his eyes.

"You've made it, my son," said Ibrahim, Oracle of Dusk… my mentor… my closest friend. "In truth, I had my doubts."

"You were right to doubt," I said, looking down at my extremities, my shame revealed entirely to this man I loved. His eyes were covered, but Ibrahim saw all, down to the most depraved profundity of a man's soul—and surely mine was carved more deeply than the trenches of the sea.

"No…" Ibrahim grasped my shoulders with hard, splintered hands, then caressed my cheek. "You are a son to me. Your failures are mine to share."

"My sins are mine alone."

The man who had become my father smiled. "Yet, here I stand."

I felt a sickness in my gut, my head grew heavy, and I collapsed into his arms. He held me close to his heart, beating in rhythm with mine.

"I've…" I rasped through unbidden tears. "I've missed you—so much."

"And I you, my son. Welcome home."

Shadows gave way to warm, scintillating light spilling through the stained glass. The walls were adorned with a polished maple veneer; a bed stood in one corner beneath intersecting planks, a cauldron hovering above a humble hearth in the other. If I had not known better, there would be no telling that this abode existed at the lowest depth of the underworld. The Temple of Abandon was no temple at all—instead, it was a home. Though I had never set foot there before, I knew it was my home, too. If only because Ibrahim had been there waiting.

"I don't understand how you're here."

"Our mortal eyes cannot perceive all that lies before us," he said, squatting on the floor and folding his bony legs. He picked up a steaming cup he seemed to have plucked from the ether and held it out. I sat in kind and gladly took the cup, pleased to smell the earthy aroma of chamomile tea.

"I am the Oracle of Dawn," he continued. "So too, am I the Watcher of the Abyss, custodian of Dysmorphia. I make my haunt at the threshold between Morgana and Grahtzildahn, and also do I reside here."

"I will not pretend to understand," I said, sipping my tea. "You have always been marked by paradox. Nonetheless, I am glad to see you."

"This is the first time we've met properly, since you were a boy."

I tilted my head. "No… That can't be right."

"You've visited me a number of times, in my hovel on the threshold, but you were not you. You were Arthur, Morgana's

Chosen. Sitting here before me now, is Cain. The boy I raised. The boy I taught to speak so eloquently."

"Do you still write, Ibrahim?" I asked, remembering the cascading scrolls flooding from the countless shelves in his scant quarters at the monastery in Skan'basan. "I imagine you have the time."

"Indeed. But is this really what you wish to discuss?"

I inhaled, a sharp breath caught in my throat. For a moment, I had forgotten my purpose for being here. Overwhelmed with the bliss and relief offered by my dear friend's presence—by the love I felt for him, the man who had accepted me as his own—I had grown complacent in my fleeting dance with comfort. I thanked the spark inside my heart for the moment of respite.

Take a breath... Now, carry on.

"From your lips, your matron commanded, I claim the sword forged from the blood of a thousand heretics." My words shattered my delusions of repose. Ibrahim's expression hardened. The room dimmed. "Do you have this blade, Ibrahim?"

"Yes." Ibrahim said, his voice strained.

"What must I do?"

The old man loosened the bandages around his head, revealing to me a vast field of stars and dust. Grasping my cheeks, he blew redolent smoke in my face. The world upended as his eyes became consumed by expanding vastnesses. As he whispered instructions, his words curled around me, then folded me in two. His voice was music—harmonious yet discordant, immediate yet distant.

I had left my body behind, my soul hurtling through a tunnel woven of nothing and everything. Stars shimmered all around, affixed in place as I traveled the cosmos at impossible speed. *Leave it all behind. Take your pain and thank it for the work it's done. Then—let it scatter to the winds. Be free, my love...*

Be free.

I felt soil beneath my feet. I opened my eyes. I was standing in a lush grove at dusk. A sycamore towered over me, taller than all others. The air was cool and sweet beneath its shade, like lingering mist after a morning rain. I fell to my knees when I realized this tree had eyes—pale, blue eyes, wind-scarred, the color of winter. They stared back at me with wry contemplation. I had waited so long to look into their splendor once more, to wither beneath their incandescence. Stasia emerged from the bark, manifesting before me in the flesh as would a dryad of myth.

Perhaps that was what she had become.

We stared at one another, my heart pounding. *Thump, thump. Thump, thump.* I mulled over a hundred scripts in my head, searching for enchanted words that might mend the damage wrought by so many cold, restless nights. Her love had been so warm, so vulnerable. It made me whole. I stared into those deep eyes, mirroring the tall mountains of her Motherland. And I wept.

My love had only driven her mad, stealing everything from her.

Stasia watched. Her gaze was not callous, but justly indifferent. She made no move to comfort me, for I have not once earned her comfort. When my last tear dissolved into the rich soil hugging my feet, I again gazed into her beautiful eyes in earnest—my heart, at peace. *Thump, thump. Thump, thump.* Around us, all fell silent. The world stilled.

I breathed deep.

"I've always put you last," I said, finally. "I've placed every duty above our family. My actions destroyed us. What I've done is reprehensible…" I choked, swallowing ash. "I am sorry, Anastasia, for betraying your trust—for abandoning you and our daughter… for leaving you to grieve the son we never met—alone. I have barred myself from forgiveness—and yet, I have come to you, asking for it."

Another eternity seemed to slip by. Her expression, unmoving. Unyielding. My insides battered by the frigid gusts of the Wyse, I had no hint of her thoughts, nor could I hope to understand the extent of her suffering at my hands.

I felt her hand fold into mine. Her bright, blue eyes had shed their cold indifference, warming to touch with a relief only she had the power to bestow. A tear rolled down her cheek—her perfect, smooth cheek, her face just as gorgeous as it was that night on the balcony, overlooking the whole of Valencia. Her dark tresses glowed, wreathing her form in a golden shroud, and she took me in her arms, inviting me in, that we may at last grieve together.

And we wept. Together. Mourning a life wasted... An eternity of pain, soon at an end.

How is it that my road has led me here? I am not worthy...

We severed our embrace. Her expression told me, *"You will be."*

I absorbed her features, layering them upon my fragile, long-molested memory. *I'll not forget you again—never again.*

I blinked. Anastasia was gone.

Ibrahim stood before me in his humble home in the lowest depths of Pandemonium. He held an unremarkable longsword, forged of iron, pock-marked from rust, polished clean. "My son..." the old man said. "You have come far."

I nodded. I have. And now, I was free of my sins.

The old man did not redress his bandages. Instead, he looked at me with his bright, bleeding eyes. With a flick of the wrist, darkness fell away in favor of warm, iridescent light. "Kneel, Cain, and be knighted once more by the light of the Sun!"

Reluctant, I fell to one knee, bowing my head before my father. My heart bounded with anticipation. *Thump, thump. Thump, thump.* He laid the flat of the blade on my right shoulder. "By the power of Dawn," he cried, the room echoing a chorus of souls, watching from the shadows. He lifted the sword, setting it upon my left shoulder. "I name you anew—rise in the light of Mourning, Syr Cain the Redeemer!"

I rose, and my father presented the sword to me. I grasped the hilt with a tremulous hand. *I am not worthy...*

Ibrahim wore peace on his face, free of the shame that had long poisoned every mask I wore. "You are worthy, my son. Dawn has willed it. You have earned it."

"Thank you, father."

"You know what must be done."

My heart was adamant, cold with righteous judgment, and set with the fury of ages. Doom tolled in the Abyss, rang along the edges of my soul-haunted blade, singing in dread tones for the time of repentance—for retribution.

"I do."

* * *

Thus, I departed the Temple of Abandon with renewed vigor, striding through the desiccated valleys and demolished ruins of Dysmorphia, following the pulse of corruption seeping down from Morgana. I walked towards the hellish sea, once an entry to living earth. No demon dared to cross my path; my way was lit by Dawn, Her light travelling through unseen realms to reach me in the depths.

I wore nothing, naked, but for the bare, unnamed blade I carried, forged of the soul's blood of one thousand men and women. Their foibles mirrored my own, and with stolid solidarity, I carried along their wretched souls on my holy errand. I carried their sins upon my shoulders. I listened to their tales and to their regrets, a legion of voices ringing in my ears, reverberating the walls of my thoughts.

Such a burden was naught but a trifle. Baptized in the light of the Mourning Sun, I was reborn. Keeper of lost souls. Guide, carving the way to salvation. I wielded a nameless sword forged from sin...

And I would use it to pierce the very heart of sin.

For the final time, I gazed up at the towering obsidian pillar of the Great Stair. The wounds on my feet reopened as I took my first step, and the sharp edges of its surface bit into my soles. But my way was lit and I chose every footfall with a decisive certainty I had never before known. Blood wept from my footprints, trickling down the way I had come—a bitter testament to my journey, forever etched into the ebon stone. My path was no secret.

The Goddess Corrupted knew of my impending arrival, and she was powerless to stop me. The Dread Angel would know her sister's divine light... and would taste the bitter tang of my blade.

* * *

The Burning City

Grahtzildahn, second layer of Pandemonium

As I emerged into the throne room of the Burning City, my old friend stared down at me with a blend of shock and elation, his vigilant bald-headed mount coiled around him. I stood before him, bleeding on the floor I had won for him, tarnishing the polished quartz that scintillated like red dwarfs in the night sky. His legionnaires moved to intercept me for fear I would dispatch their new lord as I had his predecessor.

"Leave him!" commanded Derrida from his throne. "This man marches to subdue our greatest enemy." He rose—a powerful gesture in this court—and approached me. The lines in his face went deep, and I wondered how many years had passed in my absence. "Arthur..."

I shook my head. "I am Cain. This be the name given me at birth—it is the name I carry to redeem our matron."

"Cain. Right. You walked all this way?"

I nodded.

"Well," he sighed, "you ain't walking the plains, nor the sea."

"Where is Montauk?"

Derrida grimaced. "She was shot down before you and I first arrived here."

"Her soul?"

"I captured it." He looked away. "At first, I thought to remake her old form, but Morgana's designs are well beyond my ken."

"Tell me you didn't put her in armor," I said at length, eyeing the legionnaires standing on either side of me.

"No, of course not! A cruel fate for such a magnificent creature. I had no clue what to do with her until I received this." Derrida handed me a round stone, etched with incomprehensible characters. Though I could not grasp the artifact's significance, it was clearly crafted in Old Kaldea, during the days of the First Empire. "I don't know who left it— or how they slipped in unnoticed—but I awoke one morning to find this sitting on the empty pillow beside me. My linguists and engineers decoded it; within, they found blueprints. After that, I knew exactly this gift's purpose."

The doors burst open, the air thrumming with a syncopation like a hundred iron staves striking the floor. A pure white stallion entered the throne room, presenting itself proudly before me, unfurling the great pearlescent wings of an egret that spanned the height of three men. The beast's elegance stole my breath, and I reverently offered it my hand so it may honor me with its touch.

"Cain… My dear friend."

"You have changed," I whispered in awe.

"I am unbound," said Montauk, nudging my head with her snout, her fur softer than silk. *"I am free."*

Looking into her golden, equine eyes, I silently asked: *You would ride with me?*

"Yes. One last time."

I smiled when I saw the old saddle I had fashioned when I first arrived in Pandemonium. One good memory in a malaise of shadow. I turned to Derrida, his face hardened by years of command.

"Thank you."

"Consider my debt to you paid. Just don't come back for my throne. I've grown comfortable here."

"Swear to me," I said grimly, "that you will maintain the balance. Your duty as Lord of Grahtzildahn is to stem the bleeding of Pandemonium into the waking world."

"Don't make demands in my court, Arthur—Cain—whoever the fuck you are. We've been doing fine without your prying."

I nodded, then mounted Montauk. *Perhaps we will know the taste of mortal skies,* I thought loud enough for Montauk to hear. *But first, we must earn our peace.*

Atop the back of Montauk, Dawn's sacred Pegasus, I again took to the skies of Pandemonium. The empty space between jagged ceiling and sparse, parched clouds was my haunt. My domain. For the first time, I prowled my territory of my own accord, for my own reasons. Carrying the sins of a thousand others who had not the chance to right their wrongs, I had become the Keeper of Lost Souls, Cain the Redeemer, unbound and unburdened, free to soar the skies.

We passed through the threshold barrier with ease, emerging into a raging thunderstorm unlike any display of wrath I had before witnessed of my fallen matron. As we neared the edge of the Congealed Sea, Montauk landed on a jagged rock jutting from the tempestuous waves. She whinnied and reared as I roared into the hurricane. Lightning struck the waters behind us in bitter protest. I drew my fabled sword, pointing the blade skyward. Dawn's rays burst from the tip to pierce Morgana's umbral canopy; the dark clouds scattered like shadows fleeing the light, silver waters parting for the ferrier's skiff. Thus, the heretical sword in my grip would be remade, and I named it *Scapha*.

The balance must be restored—nothing less would suffice. We had come too far.

* * *

Morgana's Keep

The Vale Betwixt, first layer of Pandemonium

"I will devour him," cried the Goddess atop her glorious throne, her voice a discordant chorus of man, woman, and child. She cast her withering glare upon the frail old man who had dared to trespass upon her sacred hall. By some miracle— rather, miraculous mercy—the Goddess did not set him ablaze right then and there.

Any reasonable man would have bowed and begged forgiveness for such an insolent transgression. Instead, the man burst into a fit of manic laughter. He hooted and hollered and slapped his knobby knees. Then he shimmied a boyish jig, all but clicking together his heels.

We courtiers in attendance gasped, whispering our speculation as to what affliction devoured his mind.

"The mystic must die," one of us said.

"Surely, he has a death wish," concurred another.

"Mad! Must be!"

We went on like this for a moment, quieting as our matron rose from her throne—a seat of power, an ancient artifact that fed us, that kept us young and beautiful. The Goddess only vacated her seat in times most dire. This was why she kept a retainer of her favored Chosen. That is, of course, until each of them abandoned their oaths.

Now, she had no one to fight her battles.

The old man leaned heavily on his gnarled stave, grinning like a damned imbecile. His teeth were foul, yellow, and misaligned. We could almost smell his malodorous breath, even from where we watched captivated in the gallery. He spewed one final guffaw before a grim veil descended over the Goddess's refined countenance, dimming the room.

"Dear heavenly matron," said he, his voice dripping with sardonic toxins. "What follows has long been prophesied. Smite me down! Shatter my soul into tiny fragments! Nothing you do will stop what is to come."

Expressionless, the Goddess said, "Your rambling is unbecoming. Your filth, untoward. I will not abide one so wretched in my court." With a careless wave of her porcelain hand, her thirty-six housecarls drew their blades. "Be gone."

Facing certain mutilation, the man's mirth remained alive and well. Miming the Goddess, he gave a foppish swing of his stave, sending a gentle ripple dancing through the air. When the wave struck the housecarls' armor, a metallic tumult rang out as all our matron's soldiers crumpled into naught but reflective cubes.

"Oh, beautiful Goddess, imprisoned so far below your rightful station," said the old, ugly man, his face obscured by the scintillating refractions of the skylight. "I cannot fault you for failing to recognize me—or perhaps you simply cannot remember, your memory shrouded by the crimson allure of your corruption…" He looked up, meeting Her obsidian gaze, his eyes alight with emerald flames. "I've cheated you time and time again! Back in the days of yore, when Dusk ferried souls down the River Acheron. Before Morgana shamed her divine sister and claimed the underworld for herself....

"Your judgement has come!" The old man slammed his stave on the floor, shattering the marble at his feet. The walls shook, the foundation quaked, sending us courtiers sprawling to our backs.

The Goddess screamed and lunged at the old man. Her ebon sword collided with a barrier of blinding sorcery, blade and spell shattering into shards of dusky glass. She raised her inky claws to clasp his throat, but something stilled her. A shadow crept across her pale face, darkening her visage like gathering storm clouds. The skylight burst open, raining lethal shards upon us courtiers. The last sight we beheld was an ashen rider diving into the throne room, atop an alabaster pegasus, pock-marked sword in hand.

As our souls evaporated, our screams joined the chorus.

* * *

Chaos reigned. Ceaseless screaming devoured my senses—whether they were the screams of my lost souls or of the gluttonous courtiers, I could not know.

Morgana unfurled her great ebon wings. She summoned a howling gale, which itself summoned a cadre of cyclones. Phrygian Black rose into the air, enwreathed in raw arcane energy nearly strong enough to contest even the Dread Angel's divine will.

The walls buckled, and the keep crumbled around us.

My spark, the lingering fragment of Dusk's soul, pulsed in time with the swollen corruption invisibly strangling the reality surrounding it. The wizard launched spell after spell, cascades of sweeping sorceries passed harmlessly through Morgana as she let out an ululating cry and charged me.

I issued my silent commands to Montauk, spinning and evading Morgana's relentless, personal assault. The Dread Angel fought not with honor nor blade, but with grotesque talons that cut into the very fabric of the ether. Storm clouds gathered; thunder shook the air, and rain plummeted like volleys of arrows.

Yanking the reins, I dodged Morgana's grasping talons, their tips grazing my throat. She feinted and instantaneously repositioned, sent a crushing knee into Montauk's chest. She laughed as my dear stallion fell gasping to the tremulous earth below, and I lay pinned beneath my mount.

Montauk!

I felt her labored breaths, the rattling of her punctured lungs.

Not again. Please.

"Worry not for me, Cain... Succeed, and we will all be saved."

My heart skipped a beat as Montauk's ceased.

Thump, thump.

My chest burned; my skin ignited. My restored body had
been shattered, and I invited Dusk's destructive avatar to suffuse
my form, to wield Scapha. When she had taken me before,
all that followed was a blur, misremembered and dreamlike.
Borrowing her strength now, of my own will, I was in control,
supported rather than dominated. I freed myself from
Montauk's limp form, and unfurled my own wings—black as
night, gleaming like onyx in the flashes of unyielding lightning.

The remaining foundation of the keep burst outward,
leaving us stranded on a sinking island. The Congealed Sea
swelled, tidal waves battering our shrinking battleground,
joined by legions of leviathans.

I felt some energy—a wicked vitality—pulsing through
the ground. With divine eyes, I witnessed for the first time the
network of bulging veins spread throughout the earth like the
roots of a demonic tree, siphoning the soul's blood from the
whole of Pandemonium—all of it coalescing at the heart of evil:
The Scarlet Chair.

Thump, thump. Thump, thump.

Morgana made a cage of her jagged fingers, dripping with
black ichor. Chanting unknowable words, weaving eldritch
sorcery, the Goddess Corrupted called upon her armies of
simpering demons that prowled the fields. Drones and soldiers
manifested around the boundaries of our holy battle, swimming
like lurking sharks in the surrounding waters.

Phrygian Black chanted in measured verse, invoking
legendary words of myth. Pascal Doon roared in the distance
as he emerged through a rent in the sky. Hordes of waterborne
drones converged, crashing into a sorcerous barrier surrounding
us—a shimmering orb, much like the wall barring Morgana

from consuming Grahtzildahn. The wizard leapt atop the back of the elder dragon. Chanting in unison, they expended the entirety of their combined potential to keep Morgana's armies at bay.

I ascended to meet her. I raised Scapha, the blade thrumming as the lost souls demanded vengeance, singing their profane hopes and wailing their disdain. Morgana, wielding no weapon with which to parry, lifted her arms as I thrust, the blade cutting through the flesh of her forearms, the point sliding through her left eye.

The Dread Angel screamed as her eye burst in a crimson mist and the shredded remains shriveled into dust. She reared, slashing like an enraged falcon. With wings of my own, I evaded her savage onslaught with ease. The crack of her wings was thunder as Morgana launched upward, wheeled about, and swooped from on high, her lone eye glinting with chthonic finality. I shifted to the side as she came down upon me, and I took from her a gorgeous, ebon wing with a back-handed slash.

Morgana sank to the ground below. I landed in front of her, consumed by a forlorn longing—the same that comes to a man when he realizes his parents were not the models of perfection he had thought them to be, but normal people bearing flaws and foibles and failures.

I leveled my blade, writhing in my grip, thirsting for Morgana's soul to join its congregation. Morgana gazed into my divine eyes for the first time. Her bleeding arms fell limp, hanging languid at her sides, her expression lifeless—lost. Beholding her hands, she saw for the first time, the blood crusted beneath her monstrous claws.

"Have I fallen so far, my love?" Morgana said, her voice singular, like that of a widow. "Have I fallen so? Even you would seek to destroy me?"

I nodded. "We both have."

Morgana's hard mask fell away, replaced with the mournful sorrow of a drunk waking after a night of blind carnage. I saw centuries flash behind her unfeeling eye, set like a cracked gem in the tarnished structure of her pallid face.

"Do what I could not," commanded the Goddess Defeated. "End me."

With a single, decisive thrust, I lunged past the fallen angel at my feet and plunged my fabled blade into the seat of the Scarlet Chair.

Thump, thump. Thump, thump.

The beating heart struggled to pump its precious fuel.

Thump, thump. Thump, thump.

Morgana wailed, writhing on the ground.

Thump, thump. Thump, thump.

I bared my teeth, twisting my blade as I pushed it deeper.

Thump, thump. Thump...

The hungry pulse of the spoiled land ceased.

The clouds parted and dispersed.

The waves and hordes retreated.

The light of the Mourning Sun touched the Silver Valley's dead soil once more, and I was the Avatar of Dusk no longer.

Finally, I was absolved of my sins.

V

From the collected journals of a mad wizard

Thus ends our tale, dear reader. With the conclusion of Syr Cain the Redeemer's valiant crusade through the warped hellscapes of Pandemonium, the Scarlet Chair's gluttonous feast of countless dead had finally come to an overdue end.

As Cain's sword, Scapha, forged from the blood of a thousand lost souls, bit into the unnatural flesh of the Chair's heart, the surveilling rains abated. The turgid waters of the Congealed Sea drained through the underworld and into the Abyss, making way for the River Acheron to once again flow through the Valley of Death.

Dusk's avatar severed her bond with her noble host and approached the Goddess Corrupted, lying twisted and malformed on the ground. Touching the cracked porcelain of her dark mirror, Dusk at last reclaimed her errant shadow.

I cannot describe what immediately followed, for I had tapped the entirety of my arcane potential and beyond—the fabric of my lifeforce was fraying at the seams. The good headmaster Pascal Doon cast one final spell, pulling us out of the afterlife and back into my quarters within the protective walls of the Citadel.

For days afterward, we awaited ill tidings, fearing the consequences such a shift in cosmic power might bring. Our fears were not... unwarranted. Word came that Mount

Vragognev, in the heart of Kuzolova, had erupted, razing the Eastern Kingdom's capital in an instant. The aftershocks were felt around the world, toppling structures throughout each of the Great Kaldean Cities and causing political and civil turmoil that took the greater part of a generation to recover from.

Shortly after the eruption, black storm clouds—not unlike those that supplied Morgana's surveilling rains—spawned in the region that was the prosperous Eastern Kingdom, one of the last vestiges of the Old Empire.

Though Pascal Doon and I scaled the Great Stair, we had not the will to gamble another trek into the underworld to see where the final steps emerged. Many have speculated that the Stair has no true outlet in the waking world; a position supported by my long-anticipated visit with Kateryna Shepherd.

I'll not forget the day I first visited my dear Kateryna—only six months after the destruction of the Scarlet Chair. I found her humble cottage near what remained of Kuzolova's western borders, a popular route for refugees fleeing the fallen kingdom to begin anew in Wystra, which had granted land to nearly twenty thousand Kuzolovii.

But time folds in strange ways, cruel ways... and I soon discovered that much more time had passed for her than it had for me.

Kateryna did not recognize me. That, dear reader, caused me profound grief. Yet, she did believe me when I told her that I had known her in another life. She had just celebrated her fiftieth year free of Pandemonium, which would have put her well into her seventies, had she lived a linear life. Her husband had recently passed away, but her home was full of spry young grandchildren enjoying their innocent youth.

As I entered, I took note of the plethora of herbal aromas. I could hear a cauldron bubbling away, releasing a comforting scent of purple deadnettle tea, which brought back memories of my mother's home in the days of the First Empire. The wood floor thrummed with the pitter-patter of scurrying children, giggling as they chased one another into the far corners of the cottage. I felt a tug on my sleeve, a tiny hand tapping my thigh. I bent down to meet my host, smiling wide to show her my teeth—all nine of them!

The little girl's face pinched. "Gross!" Lord Derrida, upon his throne, could not have issued a judgment more absolute. "Nonie! There's a jester in the mud room!" She ran off somewhere, probably into some hidden alcove to hide from her siblings. I've never been good with children, if only for my troubling appearance.

As you already know, dear reader, I've never been a vain man.

The rhythmic click of a walking stick approached. At first, I had thought myself mistaken, but I knew Kateryna the instant she spoke. "Can I help you, stranger? Headed to the fortress, eh?"

I pulled off my travelling cap and pressed it to my chest. I could hardly contain my excitement for the opportunity to finally speak with my friend in earnest—to share in solidarity all the pain I had felt alongside her.

And to tell her that she was not, and had never been, alone.

"Dear Kateryna..." I bowed, feeling foolish and utterly unworthy. "I am at your service."

The old woman's chuckle came out as a series of coughs, raspy with years of smoking. "I'm not hiring. Nor am I interested in remarrying. So, you'd best be on your way."

"No!" I laughed. "You misunderstand me—my days of courtship lie long behind. Besides, you're much too young..." I could not see what expression my words conjured, but I like to think it was one of curious bemusement. Judging by looks alone, she might have thought me a few years her junior. "I am Phrygian Black, high sorcerer and Architecton of the Citadel. I'm here because you and I were friends. In another life."

"Another life, eh?" she said at length. "Care to elaborate?"

"You knew me once by the name of Fulcrum. We worked together on the docks of Monrovia."

A shadow spread over her face on ebon wings. For a silent moment that felt like a lifetime, Kateryna looked at the rusted spear mounted above the door. She grunted, then shuffled across the room, scooting out two chairs at a dining table and lit a tallow candle. "Sit. Tell me what you know of Monrovia."

And so I sat. And I told. I recited to her much of what I shared with you, and more besides. Truth be told, I did love her. My dear Kateryna, I understood her in ways I was not convinced she understood herself... 'Tis the unfortunate foreknowledge granted to oneiromancers living vicariously through the dreams of others. I loved her, but because I understood her, I knew my love would forever go unrequited. I was no stranger to the sensation; I had fallen in love countless times in my sorcerously extended life, and I remain a hopeless romantic in my own way.

Kateryna listened with rapt attention, adding details to my stories where she could. We talked through the night, and by the time Dawn graced the sky, she was the one recounting tales. I scribbled down everything I could, recording her words as quickly and accurately as a blind man can write with an enchanted quill—which is to say, quite fast, but not as much as a seeing man with the same stationery.

In the morning, we walked her pastures and fed her flock. I scratched the chin of an elder sheep, the tenth to be named Montauk.

Together, we talked to the ancient sycamore Kateryna claimed contained the bright soul of Anastasia Cain. To my delight, she was correct—the tree was very much alive and full of conversation. Anastasia told me much, dear reader, but our conversations must remain private. That much, I promised her.

I made it a tradition to visit Kateryna every year during the summer solstice, when we would spend the nights drinking tea and wine as we talked ceaselessly. In those days, we herded her flock and gardened. Admittedly, I asked her for her hand—

more than once, but no more than thrice—and each time she declined, for Seth was her only mate. There would never be another. I then offered to take her to the Citadel to receive the Sorcerer's Gift so that she could live another millennium. But that offer too she declined.

"My only desire," she told me one humid summer night, after thirteen years of splendid friendship, "is to die peacefully, surrounded by family, who will bury me in the shade of my mother's tree. I want to rest, Phrygian. One day, I want only to rest."

When the day came, I received a letter from Edwinna Shepherd, Kateryna's eldest great-granddaughter. I locked myself in my chambers and sobbed for a fortnight, with grief for myself, and with bittersweet relief that my dear friend was finally granted the peace she deserved.

During those grief-stricken days, locked in my chambers, I cast one more desperate incantation as I drifted into a fitful sleep, consumed with breathtaking loss. I whispered the words, keeping in mind the conversation Anastasia and I had shared that sweet morning, now so long ago. I summoned a dream but saw nothing. Kateryna was forever beyond my sight.

I think of her still, and the pain remains as fierce as it was on the first night I learned of her passing. Yet, when I remember my beloved Kateryna, I can only smile my crooked smile at the fond memories of our time together. You see, dearest reader, it is the unique power of the human soul to constantly seek the good, and to live, for the sake of that good, with all the strength of the human heart...

I returned to her home and aided her grandchildren in chasing off the townsfolk, who insisted upon burning her remains in accordance with northern tradition. So too, I helped them lay their nonie to rest beneath the shade of their ancestral soul tree. Still, I cannot erase from my memory the smile locked on Kateryna's sleeping face.

When Dusk darkened the sky, shepherding home her child for the final time, and I stood alone before her simple grave, I wiped a single tear from my eye and pressed my hand against the cool bark of the tree. My vision came back to me for a moment, and I saw only light, harmony made real. Three bright souls inhabited the roots of the tallest sycamore to ever grace the earth.

And they were at peace.

Thus ends the tale of the Ashen Rider.

A Valley of Shadow

A VALLEY OF SHADOW by Lee Patton is a modern take on classic Sword and Sorcery and is available now!

For the undead warriors of The Call, existence itself is a crime, their service to the sinister lords of Enostran, a punishment. Those who disobey are swiftly destroyed, and the warriors of The Call tend to their own. Izrak Laav, a veteran mercenary of many long centuries, is tasked with the destruction of one such rogue warrior

ENJOYED THE BOOK? LEAVE A REVIEW!
&
JOIN OUR NEWSLETTER TO STAY INFORMED!